'A Journey of Infinite Miles Begins with a Small Step'

Faded Imprints

'A Journey of Infinite Miles Begins with a Small Step'

Faded Imprints

Dr. Jayasmita Mishra

BLACK EAGLE BOOKS
Dublin, USA | Bhubaneswar, India

 Black Eagle Books

USA address:
7464 Wisdom Lane
Dublin, OH 43016

India address:
E/312, Trident Galaxy, Kalinga Nagar,
Bhubaneswar-751003, Odisha, India

E-mail: info@blackeaglebooks.org
Website: www.blackeaglebooks.org

First International Edition Published by
Black Eagle Books, 2025

FADED IMPRINTS
by Dr. Jayasmita Mishra

Cover & Interior Design: Ezy's Publication
ISBN- 978-1-64560-753-3 (Paperback)

Printed in the United States of America

My beloved husband:
The lines in between speak of my sincere gratitude
for helping me realize my dream of creating this word by word.
Thanx my dear, for all that you have done for me.

Day dreaming!

Year '2000, I packed my bags to migrate to the most affluent country on earth i.e. USA. My husband got a job in NY, our basic aim for migrating was to give our growing kids a better future in this golden land of opportunities. Born and brought up in Cuttack, an ancient city of Odisha, I moved to New Delhi, consequent on my marriage in the year 1984. Moving from Cuttack to New Delhi was not that hard as after all it was within India, and I could visit my family more frequently as and when I wished. I was young and within no time I made friends with some Odia families in New Delhi, it was easy for me to fall in love with the capital city of India.

However, migrating to the US was hard and scary, we had left behind a well-settled life in New Delhi. Both of us had well – paying jobs. With very little knowledge about a foreign country, we felt like strangers and had no other option but to adjust. The initial days of settling down were difficult. My husband had a H1 visa while I was on a dependent visa without a work permit. During those days, life was not a bed of roses, we had our own setbacks and struggles. With grown-up kids, it was a very lonely and difficult life for me. I cannot express in words the mental agony I had to go through during those dark phases. Most of my writing reflects upon the strides and challenges we have faced as we gathered courage to settle down in an alien country.

With time and God's grace, things have changed, and life is good and comfortable. This land has given us the opportunity to achieve our potential. Our vision is accomplished, we have achieved the American dream, and our kids are well - settled. Blessings from heaven; today we enjoy the best of both worlds.

--- Regards and indebted to both: My country of birth and this country that has adopted me.

...Maa Tujhe Salaam!

Preface

I write primarily to vent out my inner feelings, which gives me a sense of self-satisfaction. At times, it is an obsession that has its ebb and flow. Now and then, I complete it in one go, or sometimes it will pause: with a sudden blockage of adequate thoughts and proper wordings.

At the end of each story, I send it to my relatives, friends, and co-workers. I know no one will, if I do not believe in myself and my writing. Eagerly, I wait for a response. I am confident that at least one or two of the readers will give me some honest feedback, and I bank upon their comments. These serve as a benchmark for me to climb higher on the ladder.

"Faded Imprints", is a collection of short anecdotes, mainly based on tenderness and honesty. It is all about what my heart measures and how my life is intricately woven with the values packed in serenity. These feelings have truly appeared page by page. Writing has helped me come to terms with reality; as life has confronted me with a multitude of challenges.

Within the lines of this book: I desire to honor the magic of the inherited genes from my revered Grandpa (Sri Ananta Prasad Panda) and loving Maa (Smt. Usharani Panda). They have endowed within me this gift of story writing; their magical pen gave life to everything. Their world was different with a focus on surroundings and society. They indeed had the spirit to rise and dream.

For me everything is tangible, I am a sensitive writer, and something that has touched me remains deep inside till I find words to express. My troubled mind bows to the mysteries of that artistic impulse and vision that pushes me to hold my mouse and focus on thoughts that I can recall on pondering. Mostly, the theme revolves around something that has touched deep within, it stays bubbling till it finds a way out to erupt in the form of language. I learned a lot about the writing craft because I spent so much time practicing writing with my short narratives.

I have had a fulfilling life; abiding by the ethical teachings, received from my family, and society that has groomed me. An expressed sense of accomplishment: the Lord has helped in realizing my vision. Hoping that my readers: will enjoy reading at least a part of this book if not all. -That's the greatest gift for me!

Thanx, my dear Akshay: You have been the pillar of strength behind this endeavor. Forever grateful to my elder sister, Madhusmita and my friend Deepa: For being a source of constant support and encouragement.

Feeling a sense of high!

Revealing the inner strife that bubbled deep within me:

Today, I lead a blissful carefree retired life. Grateful for the varied experiences that I have had all through my journey so far.

Fondly expressed with a bold immigrant spirit! these stories are mostly a reflection of my thoughts and real-life experiences. My strong faith in this new world has given me the courage to rebuild a life filled, with a true vision of accomplishment. My family is complete with an addition of two more loving kids: Nitika and Sachit. Today, I am a proud grandmother of three beautiful angels: Myra, Diya and Reya. Thankful for everything big and small.

I take pride in being a Woman, my life revolves within the realms of my loving family wherein I play different roles. Complete surrender -- to the Supreme Lord is my goal in life!

-Time to sit back and relax.........................

One fine day, I just thought of compiling my write ups and publishing them. This idea gave me mixed feelings:

o   Do I want to gain a Celebrity status?
o   Why do I want this to happen?
o   Is it worth taking such a calculated risk?
o   What is the basic purpose of this action?
o   What will I beget.....Cheers or Humiliation?
o   Looking back, shall I be proud of what I have done?

Slowly, I started gaining confidence within me. My anxiety level slowly disappeared. God gave me the wisdom, with time courage overflowed.

- Courage pays off, bringing measurable dividends.

Result......each page of this book has contributed to giving me higher levels of, (Psychological-Capital) – comprising of a blend of confidence, hope, optimism and resilience. I am elated!

I am ever grateful to Mr. Satya Pattanaik for presenting my valued thoughts and emotions in a tangible reading format via, "Black Eagle Books"

--------My dream comes true!!

Yeah, my book is ready for you!!! Cherish it.

Love,

Dr. Jayasmita Mishra
Email: smitamishra720@gmail.com
November 1st 2005
Ossining, New York - 10562

CONTENTS

For Maa

Dear God,
I miss my MAA, but let her go…
Maa is with u, I know!!
Bless, love and hug her tight.
Please keep her safe under your sight.
Cause, I swear by thy name…….
She was so amazing, joyful, gentle and unique
Selfless, dutiful, strong, smart and full of life!
A bundle of patience, always with positive vibes.
-She lived a contended life; well accomplished…
While the path she stepped, wasn't a crystal trail
Silently she endured all the storms, without a cry!
Maa is indeed a beautiful star in the sky.
Bereft the walls of time, volume and space
The gap between us has faded away!
Within my mind and heart, she dwells forever…
The bonding has become stronger than before.
From far and near, I can see her lovely face
Listen to her voice, feel the warmth of her presence….
Pushing me to reach higher goals, uplifting my spirit!
It's only for my MOTHER; I stand proud and bright.
I am, indeed, a part of my MOTHER: her legacy
Filled with love, she is the maker of my pathway!
Strewn with a rainbow of vibrant lights so strong.
-That for sure will last me all my lifelong……………

GOD IS WITH ME

"Spirituality and belief", in religion are the essence of what an individual is and what he can be. Our faith: defines our soul and creates a value system that make us, "who we are". I am a firm believer In God, yet I am not ritualistic in many ways. However, by upholding certain values of life and basically being compatible with people around me, I feel I am fulfilling my worldly duties in the best possible manner.

Being born and brought up in a traditional Hindu family, I am a worshiper of many Gods and can feel His presence in every matter. Moral Science, a subject taught in our school on a routine basis, has helped me to visualize the credibility in God whose miraculous powers have been instilled in us through prayers and tales of mythology. With time and age, I have understood and accepted that faith is what drives individuals into conceptualizing that there is someone guarding your actions and if you put in the required efforts ---God will help you, in attaining your goals.

When we are young and want to conquer the world, at times one is prone to be misguided, this is the time the devil takes control, and things go wary. At such a juncture, many a times, my conviction in my self takes control, I have felt the presence of something divine holding me back and showing me the lighted path. I am miles and miles away from my Mom, yet I can hear a whisper in my ear, her voice loud and clear, it is the same one that has guided and encouraged me to do my best, through all my formative years.

In a life span of more than three decades, I have seen and felt not one but many a miracle taking place as I have stepped through life's passing phases.

Moving from one end of the globe to another, I have been fortunate to witness a sea of change in lifestyle patterns and cultural diversity, each one having its own flaws and advantages. Once again, I am thankful for being able to discriminate between the right and the wrong, imbibing within me, the best of both the worlds.

I do not truly believe in destiny but Spirituality to me is "keeping one's value system and actions honest and straight in life, with the conviction that, even if something goes wrong, it will ultimately work out to our best interest in the long run".

I am not a perfectionist or a role model. I know I cannot change the world, but have learnt to appreciate and encourage the thought patterns of others at the same time upholding the basic principles and virtues of

.......Morality!

... ...I completely surrender myself to the Lord.

Hey Jagannath Meri dori tere Hath!

Role Reversal

My 77-year-old mother- is an intellectual and dignified lady in her own way. She is a great author, a well-known literary figure in society and has a whole lot of college degrees to boast. She could achieve all of that, at an age where women rarely attempted to venture College.

Past, history will talk about all the struggles that she has endured to maintain the integrity of our family, the trials and tribulations that she has had to face as she brought us up, almost single-handedly.

The best way I would describe her as, she is indeed a "Queen", with a throne made up of sharpened nails. She had access to all possible luxuries that a woman could dream of, but perhaps she was cursed and had no means of enjoying them. My father, a diligent intellectual and highly - reputed lawyer, cared and provided for her but failed to understand the finer aspects of her undemanding life. As the head of a joint family, he was engrossed in dealing with his other priorities of life as a result of which she was always relegated to the background. Circumstances made her accommodate to life's turns and twists, as she wriggled to fit into every new chapter that opened up on its own. Her inner strength and passion to build up a loving family was so strong that she withstood each and every storm.

Designer of our path, she has been instrumental in making all of us successful for what we are today. My head bows down with a sense of humility and pride for having been born to such a wonderful - Woman.

As far as her Image to me goes, simplicity is her jewel, always clad in a white sari, she bears herself with great self - esteem. Simple living and high thinking have always been her motto. With a great deal of perseverance, she has been able to sow the seeds of goodness in each one of us, today she gleams with a sense of pride and satisfaction to see all her kids grow up to be purposeful men and women in society.

I still can faintly recollect the jingling sound of her red bangles; the only ornament she wore in her hands. That mesmerizing sound: had then provided me with a profound sense of comfort and security, the fact that she was in physical proximity to attend to my childhood demands. My recent visit to her reminded me of those young days of mine wherein I led an overprotected life, which of course was not acceptable to me, I vehemently resented my so-called captivity, always wanting the carefree life that my up-to-date friends enjoyed. Believe me today, I yearn to go back to that womb of hers, lying calm within the warmth of her protected feathers. A dream which would never turn into reality! On the contrary, I pray God to give me the strength and courage that she had so that I can continue transferring the same to my kids.

Mom believes, she's independent but in reality, it takes all four of us, a ton of patience to keep this frail woman going. Thank heavens, she is in near perfect health, no pills to pop up for debilitating diseases that we have started taking, as we have balanced ourselves on the roller coaster of life. I am happy to see her reading with profound clarity the daily newspaper from A to Z. She still has the wisdom of giving each one of us a clipping of good advice that she meticulously cuts and collects from her reading material from time to time. Her memory is perfect in the sense that she would tell u in detail long tales of our accomplishments as we have grown up by the years.

My siblings, two brothers and a sister, each handle the situation differently, some with more aplomb and dignity than others. There are as many different ways of dealing with the care of our aging parents as there are people.

Staying miles and miles away from her, I am bound in many ways, restricting myself to the frequent and frantic calls that I make, the only solace for me, by being reassured that she is still there to answer my call. This of course may seem a lame excuse, the only way I can cover up my guilt.

My eldest brother, on whose shoulders God left the burden, has always had the least ability to understand or accept Mom's contrariness, restlessness and just plain stubbornness. It is his misfortune (or God given challenge) of taking care of my Maa's day to day needs. They live under the same roof. He has taken on the task with gusto, as Is his style, and has made it his full - blown responsibility to do the best job possible. Mom, however, is rarely content. It's hard to make her, " Happy". She nags and pokes her head into every single matter, giving him less chance to breathe, smothering his sense of independence, at an age wherein he has crossed the barriers of childhood. He complains that we do not share his responsibility, at times he feels desperate.

It is easy for all of us to wash our hands off the mess and say we are helpless. At best we can just pray for him, asking the Almighty to give him the strength to handle the situation with tact and passion, thereby achieving peace.

"Why can't she just be happy? I do everything in my power to make her happy! I provide for her, I pay for her care, I take her to the doctor, and I arrange everything in perfection for her. Why can't she be satisfied and contented?" The anger and frustration ooze out as he tries to strike a balance. His question is a reasonable one; none of us have an answer, we are all entangled within the strings of our own web failing in our attempt to dare solve this issue.

The truth is Mom's always been contrary. It is just a generation gap that fills this void. Her eldest son is indeed the apple of her "eye". Ungrudgingly she admits that he is the savior of her life. She is totally dependent on him, seeking shelter and refuge during these twilight years. Papa perhaps had anticipated the worst, he repeatedly had assured Maa, about this miracle "boy ", of theirs on whom she could conveniently lean.

Early on, I learned to give up trying to change my mother making it easier for me to accept and even come close to understanding my Maa's way of handling her journey into aging. Her increasing disregard for her appearance and her disinterest in socializing make some sort of sense to me. She had lost the patience to listen and had lagged behind in trying to cope with the changing times. On the contrary, her eyes light up, she laughs aloud, when she meets an old acquaintance, they pay undue respect to her, those familiar faces remind her of her good old days, giving her the status quo of a "queen "

"Why is she wearing that ratty old thing, or preserving that torn picture?" -These of course are living memories for her telling untold stories, reminiscences of her past. She clings on to a nasty old tumbler and would not even part with her tatters. Her grandfather cupboard has a big lock, with all (curios, big and small) her treasures well preserved. Strange but true, that cupboard has a bunch full of keys which she guards safely under her pillow, even when she is in a deep slumber (any bandit would suppose she has more than a million dollars' worth of goods under her control). She has a closet full of clothes!" she hardly wears, all gifted to her, from affluent relatives and friends. Mom recently said, "I have never worn such expensive clothes, now they are meaningless to me, I prefer clothing which is both comfortable and manageable. I believe this reveals her growing difficulty and lack of energy to undertake even the smallest tasks. As each day passes, even the most enjoyable activities become more and more difficult. It's a struggle for her, trying to become a part of everything wherein supposedly, others do not want her to interfere.

-What she once did easily is now monumental.

Unfortunately, we are not ready to let Mom just be who she is. It's tough to accept your own mother's aging process in all its imperfection and unsightliness. I repeatedly tell myself that it is not our job to make her happy, a truism in all relationships. That still falls on Mom's shoulders. We just have to do our part, a duty to fulfill our obligations.

My sister, her eldest born, has a better understanding of her psyche. She is the one who pampers her, looking after the details of her logical and illogical whims. She comes to pay a visit to her as frequently as she can make it. A joy to behold, such is their mother - daughter relationship! My sister once shared a great secret, "When I was a little girl, my Mummy provided me with the very best that she could afford, now it is my turn, obviously when I shop for her, I go for the branded ones only." These words have left a long-lasting imprint on my mind. She wants Mom to be with her, but the Grand old lady declines her offer vehemently emphasizing: "this is the, Taj Mahal your father has built for me I can have a restful night only in my own bed". Rather, at every single opportunity she beckons, welcoming each one of us into her loving home and hearth.

My younger brother, her youngest and the dearest one lives in another State. Situations have led him to consign Mom to a small corner of his life. He calls her up every now and then but avoids as much emotional connection as possible. He is not an unloving, or uncaring person, but there is very little he can do. He has chosen to deal with my mother's aging his own way, by bottling up his feelings. Maybe It's less painful that way. After all, he is still the "baby'' of the house, he was too young when Papa expired, shouldering his own responsibility from a tender age he stands confused, not knowing in what way he could contribute.

We as siblings and spouses struggle with how much liability we can handle and how much time we can devote to the task. As with all families, we carry our own psychological baggage and the unfinished business of any parent/child relationship. I am reminded of the famous adage:

-------One parent can look after and feed a dozen kids but when the table is turned, the opposite. seems an impossible and arduous task.

Each time I visit, I learn something new about her or myself. Spending time with her sitting and listening to her varied experiences has helped me grow, especially in understanding our affiliation. I know her better and can finally accept her for who she actually is, not who I want her to be or think she is. Sometimes it is difficult to just sit and chat when I have so many other things to do. It does irritate me when I have to hear the same story umpteen times. At times she would hold me captive, not allowing me to be out of her sight. Well, I realize that is her way of reconnecting to me after not seeing me for years.

One fine day, her eyes moistened up as she pulled me across the chair and gently whispered into my ear, "are you sure you are going to leave soon." I was dumbfounded; I realized how much she had missed my physical presence. It is but a natural instinct for every parent to pine for her child. Today, I feel the same pang when my kids have left our nest and moved out to explore their opportunities in life.

We often forget that our aging parents are still people, albeit difficult, cantankerous and certainly demanding. They have done their duty, and the reality is that we Ignore them in times when they need us the most. They know we are grown up and have an Identity of our own, nevertheless in their eyes we are still kids, and they still have the right to command, control and give us a bit of their wisdom and experience.

Sad to say, with the advancement of technology at our fingertips, we are certainly wiser than ever, not wanting to be enslaved to another's thought patterns.

Thus, continues the constant struggle for power...

Erik Erikson who Is known as the father of psychosocial development" believed that each of us passes through 8 stages of development in our lifetime. The elderly are in the last stage that he called "Integrity vs. Despair." In this stage a person looks back on their life and evaluates whether or not it was as fulfilling as they had hoped it would be. If they affirm that it was a good life, they become ready to face death. If they cannot affirm their lives, they fear death. As our parents wait for their final call, our gift as children and grandchildren is to accept their individual method of traveling the course and to take as much time out of our busy lives as we can to just be with them. Literally, we must sit and listen to their stories, to share a meal and to give them an extra hug or two along the way. It goes without saying their physical needs must be dealt with, but it is their growing sense of isolation and seclusion that can be most frightening to them, this of course makes them feel insecure and like a child they become unmanageable and ill-tempered. Isolation and loneliness can produce emotional pain as well as mental and physical deterioration.

We can go a long way in solving this problem by assuring that they are still an integral part of the family and of course by giving them due respect, a loving and caring shoulder can make a big difference.

Dwelling in the past, with nothing much to look forward, they are finding their way onto a new and unknown path they must travel alone. But we can certainly do our bit by walking with them as far as we can.

In our quest for happiness, we forget our basic duties and responsibilities; the fact remains, we ourselves are not going to stay prim and young forever. It is time for us to lead a helping hand Who knows we may soon look forward to one.

Updated scenario

--"Love begins by taking care of the closest ones-the ones at home." ~ Mother Teresa

Twelve years passed by God's grace, I could visit India more often and spend time with Maa. With loss of appetite, energy and memory, she was getting feeble day by day. I knew she wouldn't be there with us forever. Gradually, communicating with her became difficult, still it gave me solace, she was there. The positive part was that she was well cared for by my elder brother and his family, I feel blessed and thankful! Lucky to have caring siblings!

Remembering the saying, money is not everything in life, it may be partially true but in reality, it helps a lot in handling things better and bringing in peace of mind. "Money is power". For us. who live far away from our parents, the best we can do is send money home to cater to their comfort. A strong connection with neighbors, cousins and extended family would definitely help in easing the pain of powerlessness. Technology has helped us in many ways; we can harness these tools to make life smooth and happy. Sitting in my couch in New York, every day I can see and hear the voice of my near and dear ones in a remote location of India.... Built-in cameras help in keeping strict vigilance. Thanx, to science! No regrets, we can just do our very best!

Internet shopping of utilities and daily groceries is a boon in today's life, especially for aging seniors. It is easy to stock up on daily essentials at home without the trouble of getting out of the house. Staying far away, this chore can be handled well by us with proper connections with local stores who can handle online transactions.

Depending on the situation, we must take decisions that would benefit each and everyone in the family. At times, institutional care is a requisite. Rapid change in the Indian family system has given rise to the mushrooming of old age homes, which originally was a Western concept. It is high time for us to change our mindset. As the need arises, it would be more beneficial to empower older adults to be emotionally prepared for living positively with peers in a congenial setting equipped with advanced medical and nursing care. This will help to reduce the stress and difficulties of living in a home and enable older adults to experience the joys of living well with pride in their twilight years.

One sad morning, I got the news…. Maa was in a deep coma in the hospital. She gave each one of us (her children) some time to go and be at her bedside. Unfortunately, for me Covid was at its peak, the borders were closed. I could feel the numbness and sense of helplessness deep within. I folded my hands and thanked Maa for all that she has done for me. From afar, I kept praying for her deliverance and salvation.

I assumed her four days stay in the hospital meant, God was frantically looking for a perfect place for her soul to rest. Each of our near and dear ones got enough time to pay tribute to her and join in the funeral services.

Free from the bondage of worldly frame, I feel her physical presence all the more and the connection is as strong as before. I haven't seen that empty chair, so for me my dear Maa's love for me thrives from afar. It ignites the spark deep within, an eternal lightning flame! This heavenly bliss keeps me strong all along the way.

Caring for elderly parents is a blessing, not many of us get this opportunity. We would be living in a perfect society if we willingly took care of our aging parents with dignity. They did their part, now it is our turn.

Adaptability

Blame it on fate or destiny, "Chance" had it all planned, drifting along with times, as the tides tossed me adrift, from one shore to another. As a child, my parents taught me the basic secret of life -you must be willing to change yourself. Change is the only constant! In Modern management style, it is adaptability as practiced by Fortune 500 organizations. While the best means of survival is to never fret over what you don't get.

.................Time and again, I have always counted upon my blessings!

Interestingly, it was always the same remark on my report card, my teacher wrote, "with more application, capable of better results." As a young child, I never heeded these words, playful and easy-going as I was. With maturity, reality dawned, I understood the importance of being focused, perseverance and positivity worked wonders as I moved up the ladder accomplishing one step after another.

Confirming, to the definition of a "professional", I had it all set, highly educated, with a trail of coveted degrees to boast, always the topper, meticulous and sincere. Despite a gleaming portfolio, nothing worked, no matter whichever door I knocked, all efforts seemed to be futile. I was locked behind the bars of bureaucratic regulations. These posed as stumbling blocks to fulfill my career goals. Groping in the dark, fortunately, the Almighty wanted to open a window for me to see and testify it. Obviously, beggars cannot be choosers, I had no other option but to accept and groom myself in a completely unknown field of endeavor.

Less, technically speaking for sure, I am a professional, as I have gained impressive competence in a particular activity, engaging myself in a creative and intellectually challenging vocation.

My clients have immense trust in me, and their expressions boost my self-esteem. The reward may not be great in monetary terms but sensitively I have achieved it all.

I am a merchant, oh no, not of stocks or bonds, neither of expensive merchandise, I sell the whole world, mother earth sits on my palm while the various destinations hover around my fingertips. My services are legendary in the sense; they exist beyond time and boundaries.

I am a human - Travel Agent. I converse with my clients; I feel their pain and share their joy. I am not only a merchant of travel, but I am also a purveyor of dreams. As an expert weaver, I weave itineraries to suit each and every type.

My job description reads, "worldwide business/ holiday travel hassle remover. I am an enabler." People depend on me for various reasons. -- All those degrees I accumulated over the years in "Psychology", did not go as a waste. The amount of counseling I do in this job is tremendous, helping people move from one place to another. I keep track of details, an ability I might not have demonstrated as I was growing up.

With time, I have mastered this art. It has helped in giving me an edge over others. From arranging cars for pick-ups and drop-offs to finding a comfortable retirement den, everything is done to suit each one's budget and preference.

A slight mistake would upset the whole set up; I work alike a surgeon; managing the whole show singlehandedly.

I am empowered and committed to my job; the best part is that it always keeps me running ahead of time. When I am in January, I am busy planning for March and May. When in May I work for September, when in September, I check out things for December, the marathon continues, as the days pass by, years keep rolling over.

Leaving less time to whine and brood.

Business entrepreneurs rely on me, as I plan on their next business trip with great care and precision.

They have the liberty of contacting me from any part of the world. I make it possible for family reunions after long periods of gap. I am often awakened at the middle of the night, to help someone in times of death and pain. My services have helped a son perform the last rites of his father on time. I have wiped many tears by consoling and giving solace to someone who has lost a near and dear one. A dutiful daughter comes back thanking me for being able to spend quality time with her ailing mother. The list is endless, incidents like these have given a humanitarian touch with all its psychological significance.

When it comes to great ideas, nothing inspires me more than real weddings, from fixing flowers, settings and designing cakes, creative reception themes are set to steal the heart of one and all. My job is endless, as I plan out weddings and honeymoons, not only for the bride and groom, but it also includes a perfect vacation for their loved ones. With anything and everything for everyone all inclusive: from sightseeing, diving to gourmet dining, with the touch of my magic wand each moment is turned into an adventure! Honeymooners come to me for the most important trip of their lives. At times I laugh when I get to plan two or three honeymoons for the same folks. They go back and forth as it is time to renew their marriage vows. Mr. Andre was woe struck, when I could tell him exactly the color of the sand on the beach, for sure, I knew it all.

My clients typically spend far more of their time at our agency than they spend with their attorney, physician or accountant. In return, I offer them the best moments of their lives, those special weeks they have worked hard to enjoy and unwind. I plan the days that really matter in their lives. Whether it is a fun trip to Disney World, vacation to the exotic islands, cruise or safari expedition, I design lifetime experiences for them to enjoy!

I pay particular attention to clients who have retired. They have worked a lifetime to finally cherish their dreams. I make their dreams happen, as I help them, I never forget they are on a fixed budget.

The Airlines hate me for I am always an ardent advocate for my clients. Fighting to make changes and save them from paying hefty penalties to suit their never-ending demands. My educated clientele understands the leverage they have while dealing with me. As travel agents, today we are abused and have our commissions mutilated by smiling marketers of all persuasions. The media says we are "dinosaurs". The truth is that we still exist for the typical services we render.

After surfing the net for hours, people come back to me, they pay me for my services, acknowledge my worth-I am their planner, psychologist and lifestyle advisor all rolled into one.

How true were the words of my Father, long lost, thirty years back, when in business never expect returns from someone you know". The truth is that family and friends come to take advantage of your expertise for free. If at all I have gained something, it is always from unknown voices who I have never seen or met but heard on the wireless. They trust me with their credit cards as I finalize the transaction. My head bows down to all of them, who have made it possible for me to exist with dignity.

Every night as I toss on my bed, I am always dreaming about all the exotic places on this earth. Making sure all my clients are safe and secure. I have visited and re-visited all these places in my mind's eye. I suppose I could have been a doctor or a lawyer just as my other siblings are, making more money, but guess it was all predetermined. And truth be told, I would lie in bed wondering from time-to-time what kind of life I might have had if only I had gone into -Travel.

I'am part of a profession that was among the first to fight racial and lifestyle prejudices.

Our workplace is open to all, and we are dedicated to the proposition that the world will be a better place if we all get to visit one another as often as possible. With the expansion of a global economy, my strife for excellence continues, despite all adversities.

REFRAMED SPIRIT

Shivani sank into a chair and sighed with a deep sense of remorse.

I have lost 38 years of my life, imprisoned in my own home. Did I really lose all those years? Abstractly, it took me ages to build my home - a sweet family with strong bonds.

It's me; to be honest and reflective, I am a people pleaser. My basic instinct prompts me to think more about others than myself. I am always eager to offer someone my services of any kind, it is what they want praise, attention, investment -to feel valued and special. The other side of mine craves attention and recognition which involves the finer aspects of life: there is nothing more romantic or sentimental than feeling loved, noticed and appreciated. I'm not exactly proud of this demeanor- but I know I'm not alone. After all, I have always been my Mom's Thumbelina and Dad's little princess.

Born and brought up in a sheltered household with doting parents, I never had an opportunity to be on my own. To date, I have never tasted freedom as an adult.

-Marriage came with its own set of primacies, besides the normal compromises and adjustments that I had to make many a times I believed that I was literally transferred from one prison to another.

True, there is no one-size-fits-all approach to ensuring a happy married life to a daughter. The match maker made sound predictions. Our horoscopes were acceptable, and he had promised a Queen's life for me. As my parents weighed all the pros and cons, fate ensured the rest. Amidst tears of pain and joy, I had stepped out of my home to start a new life with the, 'Mehers'.

'Yuvan,' belonged to a respectable and educated family. They owned a flourishing real estate business which kept the men engrossed while we as women were homemakers. Staying at home was not a problem for me, but a postgraduate in Fine Arts, at times I yearned to catch up with my dance and painting skills which framed a part of myself. My in-lawssee the space in the word were strict and straightforward, planning and doing things on my own was out of the question.

Thumbelina was imprisoned: my passions were locked up and it came to a point where I was left with no friends. I craved for my husband's attention, time and care. He travelled for business more often leaving me behind - a cry babe. Sooner than usual, I realized Yuvan had no say in family matters, he loved his outdoor life, and I had married into a family with shackles. Afterall, Yuvan was a Mama's boy. He was not only self-centered, egoistic with a bad temper but also was co-dependent and promiscuous; soon I lost my trust. Dad seemed to have no voice, he tried to shield me in many ways and gave us some freedom, yet he failed.

It was my personality that gave in, before I could realize I became a dummy, dancing to the tune of my, "Mom-in-law's" whims and commands. A perfect fit, she commanded, demanded and silently, I obeyed. Controlling folks thrive from the safety net that they can tread on, it was easy in this case as it was an open arena. Manipulative and smart the high and mighty knew when to strike the chord. She was able to offer or revoke her affection at any time as I danced to her tune.

At first, everything around me seemed uncomfortable, in retrospect it probably helped, as I got used to the commitment. Brought up in a joint family my adaptability was better and the proximity to my parents helped bridge the gap. Each time I complained, both Maa and Papa would be extra careful to nourish within me the true virtues of an obedient child. Maa would give me an extra hug saying, "we are proud to have the "Mehers" as family, Yuvan is a gem of a boy; the power of love is infinite! Increase the dose my dear this phase too will pass." Repeated advice like this gave me no scope to develop arms of my own.

As a newly married woman, I used to struggle to understand the difference between my maternal home's lifestyle and that of my new in-laws'. Coming from a different state, it was more of an adjustment factor as everything seemed alien. From the food to the expectations and response towards me, the ground itself was shaky!

I was desperate to make Yuvan my own. His response was atypical; at times my world seemed to be spinning around him while the very next day he used to fling me out of his heart. Besides having a severe anger problem slowly, I realized he was a "Casanova", spending most of his time outside the home. Irritated, aggravated and puzzled I stood dazed. It was a matter of our collective happiness. I did not want to tarnish his image. I felt completely rejected and dejected. I couldn't talk about this to anyone. I didn't want to involve my mom or siblings as this was my family's matter. At times I contemplated suicide; fear gripped me-for sure I wasn't brave/coward enough for that.

A fair, tall and handsome Yuvan could strike a lightning in many women. I thought it wasn't really his fault the stars were to be blamed. circumstances just made it happen. I grew stronger and this gave me the courage to be grounded. Heaven gifted me with a bonus, Luv and Kush arrived to fill in the void. People with dual personality patterns know very well the act of role playing. Yuvan posed as a perfect father at home. The kids, mutual obligations, social shame, so many factors contributed, it was hard for me to break the knot. Gradually, I turned my focus within myself and devoted more and more of my time to the family, my hands were full, and I had no time for drama.

Thanx, to the social media, posting cute baby pictures on face book, looking forward to sweet comments from friends and family gave a boost to my fractured ego. I had the freedom to interact with people from all over the world on this virtual platform. It gave me enough scope to position myself in the social hierarchy and allowed me to portray a certain side of myself. I kept telling myself, this is my home, and I am the master of my own self. I used to prefer to be quiet most of the time and eventually any attempt at a conversation was reduced to monologues. The quandary had to be solved silently, and I had to fight it.

For many years, I was treated as an outsider in family matters. While I faced many emotional turbulences later in life and it was not easy to be accepted, fortunately I wasn't reduced to a nervous wreck. I was able to hold my own and realize that every unacceptable interaction had two sides to it- 'theirs and mine.' If it was important enough, I took the initiative to resolve it: otherwise, I just let it slide.

Our relationship could have gone downhill if matters were left to aggravate and misunderstanding clouded our behavior. But thankfully it didn't. As the kids grew up, the focus shifted, Yuvan became more mature, his dad fell sick for days and had breathed his last. Mom engrossed herself more and more with community meetings and spiritual gatherings.

I ventured out from home volunteering my time in the kids' school. My interaction with other mothers in the school lit up my spirit and I enjoyed the social congregations. - Life itself is tough and I didn't have to remind myself that there are many trials. Developing thick skin to withstand every storm is a particularly good thing to have; thankfully I had.

The COVID 19 epidemic came from nowhere affecting people irrespective of class, clan and color. Area counties ordered a shelter-in -place. The pandemic was still nascent, Yuvan tried to be as diligent as he could about safety in the plane; sanitizing everything he touched, wearing gloves and masks. But after noticing his senses weren't working well, other symptoms began to crop up: he felt lightheaded, lethargic and started feeling short of breath and chest tightness just from light conversation. The following day, he got tested for the coronavirus at a drive thru clinic, the results were positive.

The first reaction was fear, I prayed hard, and God granted me the strength. Yuvan was quarantined upstairs while we stayed on the ground floor, remotely looking after his needs. His cough was terrible; the fever would shoot up. Deep inside, I could feel his pain. It was tough, I had to handle things with great care, making sure the other family members remained safe.

It changed everything. For the first time I understood that no matter how much we think we are in control of our lives, the rug can be pulled from under you in an instant. I started really thinking about the act of being active and alive. My purpose was to stay healthy and become a strong support to my family. I knew I had to get up in the morning, be less tired, slog a lot, become a super Mom, supervise the business, the list was endless. As days passed, every day was a repeat of the same cycle.

This disease brought in a change in Yuvan; he started realizing my worth as I relentlessly took care of him and the household. The frustration of the nurses and doctors in the hospital taught him the hard reality of life. Unlike him, he started praying and becoming spiritual. Everything changed, the atmosphere was upsetting, yet we all strived for one goal - family wellbeing. Both of us were apprehensive; Maa had become subdued.

Yuvan was not the person he was. Living a calmer life, possessions lost their importance, his life was more fulfilled. He became less judgmental towards others, kinder, gentler, more purposeful. He felt a sense of gratitude for me as he became better day by day. Luv and Kush played an important role in becoming a perfect buffer. We looked forward to the zoom family meetings that we regularly had; the virtual platform united us. God listened to my prayers, after a few days Yuvan climbed down the stairs with a negative Covid report. He was ready to donate his plasma to make a difference in other people's lives. I smiled; half the battle was won.

As age started calling upon on Maa, gradually she experienced some physical limitations. I had to take care of this new baby of mine. I now knew my mother-in-law very well; she has always been the boss. I also saw that she did not want to be mothered. Guess no one would? I gave a pat on my back that the time had come when I would be making all the decisions for another adult, which was not an easy job.

Still very smart mentally, she had learned to change gears as needed. Finally, she started acknowledging, appreciating, and encouraging her daughter in-law's subtle and responsible behavior and benevolent acts. She had the inherent knack of being sweet tongued at her own discretion; as well as capable of being sarcastic and dominating as per the situation. However, she slowly realized somewhere in the corner of her heart that her daughter-in-law was the only one who thoughtfully took care of every little thing that she needed and desired. She was the one who never back' answered.

Thankfully, Nature gave me the wisdom to become a mother to my mother-in-law. Innately I could understand her needs: as to when to hold her hand, what to cook for her, take her to the doctor, dry her wet hair, bring her favorite fruits and so on. Eventually, she could not restrain herself from showing her love and confidence in her daughter-in-law. A victory indeed!

The years of turmoil was a perfect test for me to have trust in God's perfect timing. Forbearance is also another word for patience; you don't have to pray for patience....... It's there already! We just must release and reframe the spirit. The match maker for sure had made precise and valid forecasts. Growing up as adults, Luv and Kush have become strong pillars of edifice on which the 'Meher family's- foundation rests.

Shivani recalled her Mama's statement - "That which can't be cured has to be endured".

-"Forbearance is a fruit that will grow with your experience of being stretched in faith especially in times of trial."

-*Anonymous*-

Mom Vs. Maa

In person, Cindy is friendly, thoughtful, and giggly, a charming, blonde. A ball of sunshine, she greets me warmly with a big hug. Casually dressed in her skintight leggings and T-shirt, she flits around the home like an eight-year-old kid craving all the attention. Her calls, Mom ...mom, sounds to me like a bomb, her shrill voice keeps echoing around the walls of our home.

As per the version of all scriptures, Motherhood is magical. Going a step higher and becoming a Mother-in-law is cynical. Really, that's the only word that can describe the act of creating, raising a child and delivering it to another. Don't get me wrong-few things in life are sweeter but gradually with time they become bitter. Yes, the marriage of my son is a time to celebrate, something which I had longed for an occasion of joy and bliss. But here I stand, confused, overpowered by unrealistic expectations, and strong emotions.

I come from a progressive family, was educated in a Convent school and my parents were liberal. Sad to say, I still cling on to my logical and illogical beliefs that form an integral process of what I am today. My family means everything to me. Very deep in my heart it is very hard for me to accept Cindy as a part of our family, I very well know my limitations and keep praying for deliverance.

For immigrant parents, it is very difficult to find

proper boundaries with their children. I remember the first time I saw my daughter hugging a male classmate. I had almost passed out; I tried to provide an incredibly sheltered home environment which backfired in the sense that she became more and more rebellious. I realized, as the kids grow older, they value their personal space and do not like to be governed.

Finally, I understood that my childhood experiences are not going to be very much transferable to the Western lifestyle that my children lead. Here studies are not everything and I understood my kids would get nowhere without significant interests, passions, and extra-curricular activities. They must be a part of their clan.

I sometimes ask myself the same question not twice or five times but again and again. Have we, as parents, failed in our duty? Today, we are proud to have raised kids, who are an asset to the community. Like most parents we have just done our duty as basic caretakers and providers. They themselves have chosen their career in accordance with their choices and longing. Sometimes, it amazes me to see the way these kids have adapted to a different way of life. They are not only tough, independent, mature, and relatively more resilient to various situations but also can handle stressful situations diligently with perfection. From a tender age they have established their own sense of personal distinctiveness, which manifests exclusively in all spheres of life. They are more adaptable to changes and are less materialistic. Happiness for them is hanging around with friends in a cafe and engaging themselves with adventurous activity. Later, I assumed that as adults, their individual identity plays a much more significant role than the family identity of which I am honored.

My anxiety mounted as my son reached marriageable

age, and I looked forward to an addition to our family. My numerous phone conversations with prospective alliances gave me a new insight. Nothing seemed to work. Well, marriages are made in heaven. Well-wishers advised me to have patience. I gave up my hunt as I had no other choice. The old age practice I used was flawed.

Nancy, my co-worker, laughed and warned me, "steer clear from your son's life, it is time for you to cut the apron strings, there is little you can do just leave him alone, remember he grew up in America". I knew I had given him the very best of education, he spoke my language and loved to lick his fingers while eating home cooked food. Then why the gap? I was answerable to all my family back home who always praised me for being a proud mother. The children were polite, bright and affectionate. It was possible that we differed in the sense that our sense of perception and rational thinking patterns were dissimilar. Our arguments too had a variant scale. All attempts to reach at a favorable conclusion failed.

Sameer had a lucrative job and was sensible enough to make right decisions. True, as a kid he had a different home environment than his peers. After school, rest of the time, was spent with friends in dorms. Undoubtedly, his peer influence cannot be ignored. He is a wonder child, a unique blend of both Indian and American culture. I had confidence that he would keep up to my expectations and choose a partner as per my liking.

America is a melting pot and people from literally all corners of the world continue to migrate and call it home. While immigrants bring their distinct cultural identity along, they are expected to be "American first." It is expected that we think and act like an American, albeit a Desi American. American kids will not ask you who they should marry but will most likely announce to you who they have already decided to marry (or date or move in with). This is not because they don't value your opinion or not trust you, but rather because the most important decisions in America must be made by oneself. If you have proven yourself to be a good listener throughout their life they might ask your opinion, but in the end the decision will be theirs to make. After all, they are going to live their lives the way they dream.

Ultimately, I apprehended this truth.

Very politely Sameer would keep saying, "Maa, it has to be my way, do not expect me to marry a stranger". He would laugh and say," times have changed, give me enough time to take my own decision. This is my life; I know what is very best for me". He disliked my possessiveness and yearned to break the barriers. At first, I thought our mother/son relationship seemed to have weakened, but this opened my eyes: true time has passed while I remained stagnant. I found myself holding on to the same time frame that I had left India, more than a decade back. I was obsessed with ownership which is indeed temporary and non-materialistic. I suffered from this disease because of my own insecurity, moreover I had inherited this attitude from my parents as a part of a lineage from prosperous-so called walled families. Undoubtedly, people like this would soon become obsolete and turned off with time; I stand no exception.

Reflecting to "Indian Values," this is perhaps the most hyped issue constantly discussed by Desi parents in the West. India has changed, for the good or worse, Indians today are more and more drifting away from their roots. The fact is that the values and mores with which many of us grew up with in India in the seventies, eighties have changed. Indian

Millennials are as "globalized" or "westernized" as their peers in America or England. Middle class in urban India is struggling with some of the same challenges we see in the West: Youngsters moving in to live together, promiscuous relations, distressed marital relations divorce and so on. Family bonds are fragile, leaving little scope for higher ideals in life such as mutual help, kindness, love, hope and togetherness. Materialistic lifestyle has jeopardized moral and human values as each one steps on another's foot to move up the hierarchical ladder.

My son is adorable, smart and a doting child, like most Indian mothers I had dreamt of choosing and bringing home a coy Indian bride for him. I was stunned when he introduced me to his lady love, a chic smart blonde. He had found his soulmate, his dream girl! I had no problem with her race or ancestry. My greatest fear in their relationship was that she would take unreasonable and drastic steps, leaving him alone - wreck. Moreover, every other home is different, even though they seem to have a similar living style. The more the difference, the more the adjustment. This is because preferences and priorities vary. It was always weird thoughts like my home, my wishes, my kids, my ego, self-respect, what would people say and think that, kept haunting me. I lost my sanity!

A flash back into my own married life of thirty-five years gave me the key. When I myself, had walked into my husband's life, everything was not silky and smooth. Ours was an arranged marriage and we were strangers. In fact, we belonged to the same town, spoke the same language and followed similar cultures, rituals and traditions. Still, we encountered many phases of bickering, compromises and adjustments all through our life. As a new entrant it took me years to prove my identity with the - Sharma's.

Thank heavens, we have said goodbye to those difficult days. Today, I am happy to see a revolutionary change in the life pattern of the present generation. Happy and go-lucky as they are, they have learned to live in their own world not caring a fig about society. "Change your thoughts and you change your world." - Norman Vincent Peale. The Lord came down to bless me. I kept giving myself positive vibes, the negativity within vanished.

The most important thing is that the girl is compatible with the guy. They have been friends for a while, reciprocally there is an effort to understand and respect each other. If each of them cares for his/ her spouse's family just as they care for themselves, there will be harmony. We as parents should find happiness in their happiness and maintain care, love and respect for each other. We must be a role model for the next generation.

My eyes opened and I could find hope. My soul unlocked its windows, my heart filled with love, letting in the cool beams of reception and acceptance. I could perceive inside me a heavenly transformation. I am ready to embrace my Cinderella with open arms and become the fairy in her life. This will ensure happiness ever after for all.

........So, the Sharma's lived happily ever after.

.......An imaginary thought. Hope this story will encourage all such readers to get rid of such cancerous attachments like my wish/child/ home/ relation and so on. Unhappiness is the root cause of this. Everybody is a single entity with his/her own will and destiny.

A Gem! My Grandpa

I remember everything about you
Your voice, smile and your gentle touch
You are indeed that good soul
Who meant the world to "me"!
It was you who gave me a shoulder
To cry when I was sad
I thank thee for the comfort
Rendered in times of want!
Whilst in joy, your blessings
Paved paths to success
Your wise words till date I heed
They give me the willpower to succeed!
You were instrumental in
Building the edifice on which.
Today, I proudly stand____
Physically, though I know
You are no longer with me
Internally, I do perceive you
Keeping a watchful eye on me.
Acknowledging the bundle of goodies
You have given me
A wealth of inheritance
That cannot be subtracted
Neither spent, mined nor wasted.......
In fact, it keeps multiplying as the years slip by!

There can be no final words,
Only parenthesis, lasting memories,
Joys of sharing, loving and caring
-For each other
----All my life through
I am thankful to the Lord!
For giving me a gem like, "Grandpa"
That was, "you"!

AN UPHILL RIDE

"Pinch me! Pinch me!" The kids yelled aloud as they stepped down the stairs of the aircraft. They had reached their dreamland -America, Shilpa was excited to see the decorum and cleanliness of the grand airport. She touched one of the steel beams, they glowed, each rod intertwined with another: an architectural splendor! Shilpa had flown a long flight along with two young kids to start a new life with her husband. Amar had secured a short-term assignment with an Architectural firm in New York. The family reunion was warm, something they had longed for, and the hugs were emotional.

Shilpa was happy to be in an advanced country, which bragged about tall skyscrapers, wide roads and a disciplined traffic flow, like a fairy tale, everything seemed perfect and welcoming. Inside the taxi, the driver showed them the Statue of Liberty. He said, "it isn't just a huge statue of a lady, she's a symbol of hope and freedom for the millions of people who have migrated to the USA. The statue was the first thing they saw when they first arrived by boat and an audio guide revealed: that it was an emotional moment for most of them." Shilpa felt thankful and blessed, she dreamt of a cushy lifestyle and a promising career. Flashback something struck a chord, she realized they were in a foreign land, leaving behind all their relatives and friends in India. Breathing in the fresh air, she could feel a mixed sense of fear and joy at the back of her mind.

Cutting a long story short, days passed, things changed. Adapting to a new way of life in an alien atmosphere had its own drawbacks. Everything was not as bright as the initial euphoria was. Even simple things such as kilograms/liters and kilometers needed serious revision into pounds/gallons and miles.

Shilpa missed home, the daily buzz of a busy metro life in the capital city of India. KARMA- Let's face it; the family geared up as a team!

Amar, a workaholic was engrossed with his job and future career prospects, the kids were in school trying their very best to be a part of the milieu. Shilpa felt a sense of void within her; she understood that her hopes and dreams were far from reality. Landing in the land of liberty, the lady with the torch mocked at her, without a work permit she could not even apply for a job, all her attempts to utilize her educational qualifications failed. Sitting within the four walls of the home was not her cup of tea, so she decided to do volunteering.

Public transport in the suburbs was limited without driving skills getting around the town was not easy. Keeping in mind the limitations of commuting she decided to volunteer in Amar's office. The office premises were nearby, the people were familiar, and this would give her an opportunity to get out of the home and refresh her computer skills. She knew it would be difficult but was ready to push her limits a little bit too far.

Amar was one of the corporate leaders while Shilpa sat at a desk performing basic duties as an assistant. "Dignity of labor," that is what they say, never mind she was happy: this was a perfect arrangement to set the ball rolling.

When she was in third grade, Shilpa was familiar with bullies in class, she kept a safe distance from those rotten apples. Reality dawned when in this office setting, she encountered people projecting negativity and back-biting traits even as mature adults. Insecure and fearful people display such traits where the work culture is based on the dictum of....". Hire and fire". What else could one expect from people who were shallow and rootless? The atmosphere was full of rejection. However, for Shilpa, her adamant and defiant attitude taught her to be her own advocate and stay grounded.

.... Unfortunately, things did not work out in Shilpa's favor.

---"My first instinct was to let them go their way and I would go mine; thus, the situation would be well managed. I have never killed an animal I was not obliged to kill; the sport in taking life is a satisfaction I cannot feel. Yeah! This seemed to be even worse. I knew very well that I was the target for something else. I took a deep breath, closed my eyes and remembered the prayer, which we did every day in school. "Oh! God our Father forgive those who do evil. Give them the wisdom to distinguish between the good and the bad. May peace prevail on earth- Amen."

Difficult times are those that help you recognize the best of friends. This time Shilpa was extra tough, perhaps she had anticipated the worst. The phone stopped buzzing, friends never asked about her absence. Everything seemed to be so normal as if nothing had been affected.

"Are you crazy? I feel you need to get yourself checked by a psychiatrist," said Amar as he saw the changed Shilpa. "You and the sacred book, stop chanting those prayers and prepare yourself for something more worthwhile. You are blackmailing the poor Lord; you never thought of Him before and suddenly you have become such a saint".

A stimulus always provokes a response. Circumstances determine one's behavior pattern. Shilpa very well knew that she would never be able to fight alone. It was indeed a deal of seven is to one. She also knew that realistically it would be hard for her to demonstrate the truth to the world that she was innocent. It was indeed very hard to believe, things had definitely turned upside down for her.

Everything seemed to be so uneasy right from day one. Her voice sounded shaky when she revealed the fears that lay within her heart-" I know I am treading on a dangerous path, but I am sure they are not going to hang me". This seemed to be the last resort for her, and she didn't hesitate to give a trial.

Amar kept reminding her to be extra careful, as it was his dignity that was at stake. It was by sheer diligence and hard work that he had achieved his goal, and he did not want anyone to point out to him because of any lapse on her part. Any slight mistake would reflect on his competency and caliber.

" I am not an idiot," thought Shilpa," I have the brains to learn, and I am sure nothing is hard if one has the will to achieve." A strong believer in God, "I find ways to love myself. I pray, meditate, drink lots of water, take a bubble bath, walk on the tread mill, listen to music and at present have learned to hang out with a bunch of friends, based on their basic integrity."

Amidst a cold and stifling atmosphere somehow or the other her survival instincts worked hard to fight against all odds. She found within herself an invincible sense of warmth and learnt the job within no time. "Who has the time to teach you, the big boss must be mad to hire such a dummy without any prior experience". These were the words she had to digest, but it was better to tolerate rather than create an issue.

Day in and out she worked hard to please the rest. Weekends became working ones as she had to rake up a huge backlog. Stress piled up, but it was ok at least the time seemed to fly off so fast and she did not have to sit and brood at home. Days, weeks and months flew off, fast and she somehow or the other tried to become a part of the furniture within the office decorum.

It was summertime for the kids and her best friend as well as her co-worker planned a trip to go to her native land. "Do not worry, Renu, Shilpa assured her, go ahead and have a nice break, your work will be well taken care of." Nature has its own way of taking care of its various functions, in the absence of a part; If the left hand is broken the right one takes up more load to achieve the optimum.

Willingly, she volunteered to take up Renu's job while others merely washed their hands off. Though it was hard, she somehow or the other managed to do it.

Oh! Not a word of appreciation from her immediate boss for she never seemed to be satisfied. Like the wicked witch's story, the more she accomplished the higher was the expectation!

Every evening it was the same story at home; a tired Shilpa had very little energy in her to attend to the multifarious jobs that had to be done back home. In fact, the slightest complaint about her work atmosphere would ignite a spark, sufficient to have bickering's between the couple and thus nights used to pass with each other ending in separate bedrooms. Amar never ever seemed to understand, as a good Samaritan he always found some fault or the other in his wife rather than realizing the cold environment where Shilpa had to struggle most of her time. Perhaps, he seemed helpless in helping her out and at times used to scorn at her- "Learn to survive within the dirty politics of a work atmosphere."

Alas! Fate had willed it differently. One fine day, the boss ordered her to help Peter with his job. "I have never done that kind of work," said Shilpa, and "I still must finish my own", admitted the perplexed Shilpa. The boss retaliated by saying, "you could defer yours; Peter's job is a priority, and the head has given orders that your language seems to be good and so you could handle them in a better way." Instances like this kept happening and no matter how much effort was put in, things never worked out in Shilpa's favor.

Days rolled on and on - when things started taking a bad turn, she had to admit defeat and descend the arena. Shilpa was asked to stay home, officially she had lost the job.

Today, she sits brooding into a vacuum trying to gain enough strength to move along her dream ladder; heavy at heart still, trying to reach her goal-of self-actualization.

Perhaps she was destined to be a sinner, with no means and ways to get out of the trap, groping in darkness a dazed Shilpa tries her best to plead for innocence a myth that would never ever turn to reality!

With folded hands she thanks heaven-"Lord, I am happy Amar is saved, I take pride in his growth, let him bloom and blossom while I remain a shadow beneath his strong shoulders. I am a woman the queen of his heart, home and hearth. Our happiness lies in mutual understanding and respect for each other's dignity."

-He could never tolerate her exploitation that too right under his nose. That's how fate played its role in ending the torture.

DIVINE BLISS

FAITH can move mountains. Passing through different phases of life we have faced difficulties which many a times have a miraculous ending. This itself explains the existence of a Superpower. Here is one such encounter I had faced, that had a happy ending.

This happened on a snowy winter evening in New York. My husband was returning from an official trip from Brazil; he called me up from Miami. I did alert him about the bad weather conditions in New York. I suggested that it would be better and safer for him to stay there for the night and catch the plane the next morning.

I now realize, his eagerness to come home was quite strong, his immediate reply was that if the flight flew to NY, he would definitely take the flight. As the paradigm goes: Men seldom listen, for sure the flight reached LaGuardia Airport with a lot of difficulty. Technology helps; all the time I was busy tracking the flight and my anxiety heightened when the plane kept hovering above the airport as the snow was being cleared by busy workers at the ground level. Twenty minutes, it encircled high up in the air till the runway was shoveled, and it was safe to land.

The phone rang, I was relieved to hear Parth's voice, only a sailor's wife will understand my turbulent mind and gamut of emotions involved. This time when I spoke, once again I pleaded with him to book a hotel and stay nearby rather than risk coming home, which on normal days would be an hour and a half drive. Stubborn and firm, he was determined to take his own decision. At the airport none of the cab drivers wanted to give him a ride. Exhausted, frustrated and drained out, he ultimately reached the train station in our town using various means of public transport, a shuttle, bus and train. At the train station again, it was difficult to find a conveyance home, no cabs were available.

Our efforts of getting help from neighbors and friends also was in vain. I tried calling a few friends, the irony: it was always the voice message answering my call and I had no patience for that. Times are different, no one wants to be bothered about other people's crisis. They fail to understand that it is always a two-way street. One small gesture of kindness or good deed can create a domino effect of paying it forward.

Panic stricken, I decided to seek help from neighbors, whom I knew for the past fifteen years, by virtue of residing in a huge apartment complex. Every other day we met at common places; elevator, lounge, parking lot, garbage bin, recycle area and so on, not forgetting to exchange greetings and smiles with one another. After all we shared a common sense of affinity and bonded as a big family.

Cutting a long story short, at times your own people do not realize the gravity of the situation and back out when in need. It was hard to believe that the neighbor who had a 4/4-wheel drive van, could have helped but he was so engrossed in watching a movie that he bluntly nodded his head and literally slammed the door on my face. Probably he was enjoying his, "ME" time to the brim. A police officer whose duty is to protect people also shrugged his shoulders off. A friend and good neighbor refused, explaining his own limitations. It was a period of intense stress, I felt helpless!

Cold and annoyed, Parth decided that he would walk home. My heart missed a beat as I knew it would be an arduous task as he had his heavy Baggage too. Not to mention he was sick two months ago and was under strict medical supervision.

I had no other option: just closed my eyes and prayed. I decided I would also walk down to the train station so that when we meet both could help each other. I was just getting ready to go and lo behold! I opened the front door, to my utter disbelief, Parth was standing in front of me. Indeed, this was a miracle. It so happened, an unknown Spanish lady who had gone to pick her family from the train station, did offer him a ride and dropped him right in front of our building. Swearing on God's name Parth said he never knew the lady and from nowhere she came beckoning him to sit in her car and dropping him at his destination. Everything appeared to be well planned; she was God sent.

Angles do exist on earth, immediately I could visualize myself under the protection of being in God's care. An unforgettable experience, worth sharing, prayers are answered; for sure miracles do happen. We should all recognize that every time God does choose to perform a miracle in your life, He is showing you, His love for you in a tangible way.

---I trust in the Lord, the supreme power: He is my savior!

UNFOLDING MYSELF

A few things I had to boast about: on top of the list was my close-knit relationship with my sibling - Chetan. It was evident, in each action of mine, that I cared loved, and looked after my only sibling, my younger brother. Like, two peas in a pod, we grew up and blossomed into wonderful adults under the umbrella shade of our doting parents.

Five years apart, he was a lively doll for me. My first lessons in caring and sharing started with "Laddu", the way he was fondly addressed at home.

Our Bal Gopal: Krishna Kanheiya, "Laddu'. As a kid, "Laddu" was pampered and spoiled. All the elders, including me, gave him undue importance. We all cared for him to such an extent consistently, that he failed to learn basic tasks that he could do himself. Between both of us we played all types of games be it an all-girls' game like, hopscotch or a boys' game such as, cricket. To make him happy, I would always pose as a loser. Today, as we stand upright and strong with gray hairs and strong shoulders to lean on, he excels and has a thumbs up, an edge over me.

Since he was a precious son, I was an indispensable figure, he was born after me (the lucky charm). The most important mission for me in my childhood was taking care of my younger brother. When I think about it now, since I was only five years older than him, the request of adults to take care of my brother was probably from their hope that I would get along with him without fighting.

- Unforgettable indeed those good old days. That crybaby with chubby cheeks and the cute thumb-sucker was always an ardent follower of mine. I was in the third grade when he joined my school as a kindergartener. He would come to school with me after much ado. The ride was fun and ok, but as soon as he was in front of his class he would start crying and never get inside. Our helper Raghu would guard him outside on the grounds till school was over. As seniors, we had a forty-five-minute extra period and happy Laddu would come to my class and sit near me until my class was over. The funniest part was that he used to sit quietly like a mouse (an odd person in the class). I still wonder how he was allowed to do this in a school with strict rules. I believe; this is how he finally learned to sit in his class.

My surroundings were such that I became more mature, competent, and responsible with clear and realistic goals. On the contrary, Laddu derived satisfaction from fantasy; and was stuck in 'me' mode. "Everything revolved around his needs, concerns, feelings, wants, desires, and everyone else took a second place in his life."

Growing up, I remember never fighting with him for anything. Very early in life I had learned to give in and protect him under every condition. We did enjoy playing pillow fights quite often and at the end, I made sure his pillows were securely tucked from all sides while sleeping in case he rolled and fell off the bed.

Over the years, memories slowly fade, but some incidents here and there remain fresh......

It was a lazy warm afternoon; I was busy painting

a card for my favorite teacher for Teachers' Day. Laddu came from nowhere and messed up my colors. He thought it was fun, but I got enraged and shouted at him. Not realizing the damage he had done, he kept laughing aloud, which irritated me even more. Not used to being bugged, he picked up a hairbrush and angrily hurled it at me. The brush hit hard on my forehead, and it hurt a lot, not to mention the reddish-black bump that it created. I remember that was the first time I had complained about him to my mom as pearl-like tears rolled down my cheeks. Mom, took my side, she started scolding him and wanted to beat him up.

Lo! I was there for him, standing in front, shielding my Laddu from Maa's wrath. Those precious moments of love are imprinted in my mind's eye till date. Laddu's friends were mine too, I always did my very best to see that his friends had a good time, and yummy snacks were served whenever they came home to play.

Laddu had access to all types of luxuries that an affluent kid would dream of. He could never stand the word; "refusal" or "no". Adolescence: was the chapter that messed him up. He started throwing tantrums for no reason. He disobeyed elders and was least motivated to do scholarly work. His poor self-esteem and bad company gave rise to bigger problems. Frequent anger issues were predominant, and he went out with friends to drink alcohol. He would disrupt the whole house if things did not work as per his will and demands. It was hard to appease him; the only son of liberal parents he had his cake. All his wishes were fulfilled.

He graduated High School with not very great grades, yet Dad gifted him with a four-wheeler. Not only could Dad afford it, but it was safer for Laddu to ride a car, than a two-wheeler. No one could bar him from not having a nightlife out with friends and it was scary!

As we grew older, we stepped into the world while fate played its role in shaping our future. I moved with my husband to the US, while he led a luxurious life backed by the financial assets of my father. This was the time; I could feel the difference. Soon, I became a rival. As per legal status, we both shared equal rights on parental property. The very thought of division was out of the question, he yearned for all.

This rivalry and possessiveness did increase as he grew up. Our relationship had become so bitter that I had stopped communicating with him. With time, Maa passed away leaving my father a mental wreck. Laddu took advantage of this situation and transferred most of the property into his name.

God's grace, there was no need, but I felt cheated and there wasn't much I could do or say. Monitoring and looking after Dad's failing health was no easy job without the cooperation of my only sibling. That job finally ended when Dad breathed his last. - A void was automatically created.

Fast forward, we remained busy with our own lives. One fine day I found a message on my WhatsApp from my dear Laddu. It was a mixed feeling of joy and apprehension. That one small message was loud enough to crack the ice. I cried, my eyes welled up with tears, he wanted me to come to India to settle some other tangible and intangible property matters. They needed to be consolidated. Without my signature, they would not be easy to liquidate.

My inner voice spoke: As a legal heir to my parents'

hard-earned assets, me and my kids would love to have a share. I started planning to visit India and sort out the matters in the best possible manner.

- A man's heart devises his way: but the LORD directs his steps.

I eagerly responded to the phone call I received from Laddu's wife. In a miserable tone, she gave, the sad news that Laddu was admitted to the hospital and was in the critical care unit. He had suffered a heart attack.

Words failed to express my feelings, after all, he was my blood.

I had no other option but to pre-pone our tickets and fly home. I arrived, just in time to say goodbye to my little brother. All bitterness that lay within vanished as he fondly touched my hands. He then looked at his wife as if he wanted to say something. That was it, and a spell of darkness engulfed us. Grief added....I could finally just visualize him as a part of myself. Decades of misunderstanding and distance were chipped away in the blink of an eye.

"During life's highs and lows, hurts and happiness, a sister is always there."

- Catherine Pulsifer

I had no time to think; the stark reality of life glared at me. Those eyes of my little brother pleading to take care of his family. Two young kids and a devastated sister-in-law; for sure they needed me.

I was the lone survivor, with none of my own kith and kin alive. I stood at the altar praying hard. The association between age and wisdom is intuitive. Yes, I was always a responsible child with a concrete awareness of the relativism of values and priorities. My inner self seemed to unfold, I started to believe in myself, and those belief systems were accurate oozing out from deep within.

Reflections of my childhood days gave me an insight into acting rationally and reasonably without bias. As a student of Psychology: All the basic cognitive/ reflective/affective dimensions of Life's reality seemed more apparent.

The rest of the days were spent running from one post to another pillar, rummaging through old papers and files. Scrutinizing long-lasting documents and coordinating as well as arranging meetings with lawyers, chartered accountants and bank managers. Time flew, and angels from heaven supported me in my mission to do my best.

Those busy days were over. Shortly, I was at the airport, bidding a tearful goodbye to my sister-in-law and the two little kids. I thanked God, for having the wisdom to regulate my emotions in a rational manner. All these years, staying away from my near and. dear ones has given me enough procedural and factual knowledge of life. I have done my part. Every step was meticulously planned, with a profound sense of awareness of the relativism of values and priorities keeping in mind the context of human life span. This, in turn, has given me the ability to recognize and manage uncertainty. God blesses!

--"When the light returns to its source, it takes nothing of what it has illuminated".

-Anonymous-

PASSING ON THE LIGHT

The phone rang at an odd hour, conveying me the sad news, my big "B", uncle was no more. The news wasn't unexpected, every time in my thoughts: I had prayed for his deliverance. We do miss his physical presence but feel relieved that his suffering has come to an end, Living, far across the seven seas; I could visualize the family gathering at, " Kalyani Bhawan", the ancestral home of my grandpa; which literally was the "Disney Land", of my childhood days.

Magnanimous at heart, compassionate and sensitive to fellow beings, he left behind a legacy of treating everyone alike despite differences. His excellent communication skills were commendable; that made people of different backgrounds comfortable: they would relentlessly talk and discuss important and complicated matters in detail, irrespective of their age and profession. A pillar of strength for a large joint family, he had instant remedy for any problem that would crop up from time to time as he was the sagest of all. He knew how to see only the bright side of life and almost took a childlike pleasure in doing most things, big or small.

An epitome of Lord Rama, he performed his household responsibilities with great tact and perfection. My grandparents were fortunate to have given birth to such a great soul; He remains an exemplary model for one and all. Any kith or kin who came to him would be given due honor, a rightful place in the home and hearth.

The other day, I was narrating in detail to my kids about, how he used to ask us to push him up the stairs from the back like a bull dodger, as he always complained that he was too old to climb up the stairs. A relaxing Sunday afternoon, after a sumptuous lunch, we cousins would clutter around him, listening to stories and adventures that he would narrate. We were awe struck as everything he related was new and filled with exciting activity for us. His deep sense of humor, coated with love and care for us is deeply engraved within our mind's eye. Literally he gave us the quality time that we always longed for.

He invented his own cordless phone; by attaching a lengthy chord; we gladly carried it all along as per his will. For a meager two paisa per hair, we would meticulously sit down plucking out all his grey hair, while he would snooze and sneeze as he dozed off after his midday meal. He liked to sneeze, a strange yet humorous pastime by tickling his nose with dried neem twigs- that was my "Big B uncle",

He loved to watch us play hide and seek, chor police and kabaddi. He taught us the basics of football, cricket and hockey. From cycling to swimming, he was our "guru". We enjoyed playing all types of games under his supervision. Recollecting those days when we would dress up in new clothes and perform all the rites and rituals of various festivals with him, while my aunt welcomed all of us into her benevolent arms. The long summer days were spent in the garden, picking mangoes and berries of different types. He never forgot to reward us for our good deeds and punish us for the wrong ones. A unique human sample of, "righteousness".

My little ones have grown up fast, they have so many

queries, for they do not understand as to why Mama cries her heart out for someone who she does not see or hear so often. Their naïve minds do not visualize my bonding of past years, for they have only to cry over I pads, laptops and I phones.... Not for human souls.

They do not feel my pain, for them relationships are limited, wish I could give them something more in life than what they already have, like a mad person, I try to instill in them the real-life values by narrating my rich heritage.....

My big, "B", uncle has indeed lit a candle, for all of us to follow, he did it, he received it....let this light move on.....a torch of compassion filled with unbridled love!

....."Your life was a blessing; your memory has immense value. 'You're loved beyond words and missed yonder treasures"-A tribute to my eldest maternal Uncle, Mr Srikant Panda. (ex-MLA, Cuttack)

RECONCILATION

When you're looking for love and I was-you try everything. For years, I followed the advice of friends, associates and self-help authors but no one could reach the crux of the problem. Yes, I have failed, and my failure means his also. It takes both of us to save our married life. Yet I can't tell you how many times I clicked off the music system in the middle of a love song and burst into tears because I lacked a relationship to sing about. A chubby baby's giggle, a pregnant lady waddling like a duck, a proud young mother trudging along with a stroller, a seemingly happy couple, a sweet sacred home and all such similes were strong enough sights to spark a trickle of tears in my eyes. Yes, I was jealous of them and could feel the pain within. At this point in life, I had indeed reached the backside of twenty and in quest for some stability and meaning in life.

Family and friends say I'm a good catch. A smart gentle attractive woman like me seemed to be the ideal and compatible partner for my broad-shouldered handsome Vivek. Yes, today the same Vivek seemed to be a mental pathology, with a trail of unflattering adjectives that my mind could tag him with-"silent", "selfish", "brooding", "uncommunicative", "emotionally barren" and last but not the least a nincompoop of the first grade, spoiling his life for other's sake. He had lost interest in me, and I could see, hear and sense that I had become a mere image of dollars and an item of trade for him.

Our relationship remained limited only to the boundaries of the rent that I would pay him at the end of each month and the services that he expected me to fulfill at his will, that too within the closed walls of this home- that smothered me to death. I knew very well that he was abusing me, and his gestures definitely served as doses of slow poison.

My parents lived close enough to support me, I had a well-paid job to lean upon, but the path to this home seemed to be my destination. Every evening, my car would head back to this place wherein lay my heart and hearth. We lived here as roommates; he never ate from my hands, and I hardly cooked for myself. Yet, I take pride and solace in calling this place my home-for in the eyes of one and all we were -Man & Wife. My tired body would always lay down calmly on this bed where I have learnt to sleep alone.

The sweet innocent little girl of the neighborhood once had mustered up enough courage to ask me a sensitive query-"why can't you have babies, like others do"? "May be, God never willed it for me as he seemed to have other plans" was my prompt reply.

Reminiscences behind had always spoken of the good times that we had shared together, the happy moments that we had witnessed-all seemed to be dreams that would never ever materialize once again.

My man Vivek was robbed, oh! no, not by another woman but to his brother's wife who seemed more important to him than me. Back home in India we know that a woman is married to a family and not to the man alone. It is true, that I am no longer an Indian as on legal terms, but in deeds, thoughts and words I do possess the same traits that were imbibed within me during the growing years of life where I had spent most of my crucial stages of growth and development.

Madhuri, his brother's wife cooked cleaned and ironed for him. His paycheck was passed on to her and she seemed to gain some sort of sadistic pleasure seeing me unhappy. She possessed the wisdom to have two men dancing to her tune. When not in harness his hours were spent entertaining himself amidst their family within which he revolved. Baby Esha seemed to be fulfilling his fatherly needs or maybe a man would never crave to be a father as would a mad woman like me, who always yearned for a babe made up of Vivek's blood planted and nurtured within my very womb.

Weekends were times when I would ignite my spirits hoping against hope that something concrete would crop up and I would once again win his heart. Efforts to please him were in vain. Our relationship always ended in between a bunch of tangled wire that would trip me up. At the wee hours of the mornings, Vivek would be mine and with the rays of the sun the push theory would work dragging him out of the house, leaving me lonely, desperate, desolate, and whining like a street dog left out to fend for himself. Nothing seemed to work, and I would end up cursing my fate.

One fine day, he told me that he had taken the decision to move out while I ought to think and plan my life goals. These were his final and ultimate words; and I was aware he would be rigid. I ended up being cranky, after sleepless nights, restless as I would feel; even the sleeping pills stopped working. I sat upright in the middle of the night, I muttered to myself -Vivek, very soon I would be losing you. Let's decide on something more worthwhile, another big chance to make up. However, the deal was always with me to give in to his unrealistic demands while he never was in a mood to compromise. In my eyes he was always at fault. I closed my eyes and thought for a while the problem was "Vivek", but in reality, I was robbing myself of the power to transform the situation. Because while you don't have control over what others do and think the one person you can change is "you". I seemed depleted off all my resources, my mind could think of nothing else to heal up the wound, like a wounded tigress I lay in bed tossing all through the night. He seemed to be a stone, sick at heart and weak in mind.

The sunshine glittered on the dust, gathered on the photo album that had cherished memories of that important day of our life when he was my Prince charming, and I was his Dream girl. Today, they remain untouched, remnants of the memento of our rusty relationship over a relatively long time period.

Divya, this is not a relationship to give up, think hard-will you be able to adjust to another stranger? And who knows that person might be worse? Would you be able to live the rest of your life alone? Yeah, you are lucky to be living in a free society where no one bothers about anyone except their self but again do not forget your roots. Will you be able to forget this Man of your life? The guy with whom you have lived for seven whole years. Is your heart ready to take the ultimate decision? Will you be happy after breaking this relationship? The walls echoed around asking her the same questions again and again. The furniture around seemed to laugh at her-these were those which both had taken great care to choose, buy and set in accordance with their heart's desire. Friends, family and the rest would always be there -but remember -Divya-you are the one to face the real consequences.

As if awaking from a reverie the reality dawned -better late than never. Going by the collective adage, "All men are dogs", or looking at the individual person you're dealing with, it's so much easier to blame him than to ask yourself, is there something about me that I haven't looked at yet? The truth is, when we want a relationship with a man who isn't ready to love us fully, it's a signal that we, also are not ready and there is still some more scope for adjustment and amendment. Whenever he was in a mood of getting emotionally intimate, I knew I used to pull away, sometimes I did even yield and that was when I too needed him. Raged, irritated and depressed at times my independent woman persona would become prominent and "I'd say," I don't need you and you are expendable", but the truth was it was always from the mouth and never from the heart. I remembered my friend Mita's words: "My husband thinks I am a fool, he just takes me for granted and always tries to find fault with me, but I know underneath his tiger skin is a baby lamb whom I can manipulate. In spite of his harsh outer, he does have a heart that melts like cheese; deep within me, I have the faith he would never throw me away and would go to any extent for my sake -be the need." Not all men are same. You wouldn't think it would be hard to let a man do things for you, but for me it was", says another friend, I know. While there are other lucky ones: like Rekha, Mona, Anu, Shova and the rest who behave like a queen and are fortunate enough to have their men at their beck and call.

"Maybe, I was somewhat different, made up of all steel and iron and thus had to bear the burnt. Being a self-sufficient woman isn't a bad thing, living in this country has taught me to be self-reliant in many other ways that his traditional bent of mind failed to appreciate, but that doesn't rule out the fact that I did not need Vivek as my life partner." The woman within me started craving for that idol which very well I knew I had lost. "Baby, I got this!"- if indeed a man feels he has no place or purpose in your life, he has no reason to stay there.

For me things seem to be more difficult: will I be able to tolerate him with another woman in his arms? How far can I go out of his life without meeting him at any point? After all, we live in a small world. Suicidal thoughts at times overwhelm my imagination, but that too seems scary, one has to have the real guts for that, and I knew I was weak. "Divya, do not give up!!!" chuckled the little girl of the neighborhood as I sometimes used to speak out my heart to her. Her naive mind also could realize my agony and the need for support.

I was determined to do something, and I knew the keys were in my hands. I realized that my sense of insecurity and senseless ego was the primal force that tried to end our relationship. My negative mind-set and faultfinding attitude that took hold of my reins drove me towards bad behavior; it injured me most and the anger remained taking less time to fade. This all resulted in chipping away at my most cherished relationships. As I have traveled through life, some shadow of myself has added color to my true image -in all my moments at the conscious, subconscious or unconscious level they have been revealed in the dual form of joy and pain. Truly, I have been operating with negative feelings brought from another time and place, associated with a whole separate set of issues. I gradually learnt that one cannot create anything good with leftovers from the past. The therapy as suggested by my Psycho-pal lay in healing the past wounds that keep hurting you and to step back from living on the edge to quote her very words: to leave that dust ball in the corner and go to bed, thanking the Lord for the good day that had passed.

When we're sweet to ourselves, we're sweet to others. From an unhappy place nothing satisfies. We see clearly that we are born to love, not to judge and that it's not our job to fix anyone. We all have the right to live our own lives and learn our own lessons. When your fellow beings do not take the right path, it's only because they don't see it yet and if we can there is no harm in leading them forward.

Relationships offer the greatest opportunities for learning and growing at whatever depth we choose. I have learned the hard way: I will give in because I cannot afford to lose him and no matter how he behaves, unconditional LOVE is what I will give, that's the only weapon that would ease my pain and end my suffering.

A smile on her face, twinkling eyes, added with dimples deep, Divya remains determined in her will to win. Time has taught her to have faith in Him, who makes each one of us perform on His stage. She has learnt to count upon her own instincts to better understand her hubby's mood swings and dance to his tune, each moment passes with high hopes, for one can only do one's best.

Stressing on his positive approach while negating the irrational moves has made her a happier soul. She realized the fact: nobody is perfect, nor completely correct. Finally, at the end affection is always greater than perfection.

- Enjoying, rather than enduring his sarcastic and eccentric ways, has paved a path for improvement and things have started working in her favor. A small step on his part serves as a giant leap for Divya. Relentlessly, her effort continues as she successfully saves each and every twig of her battered nest.

-"God apparently created Eve from Adam, to serve as a support on which rests the edifice of strong family bonds. Marriages are indeed made in heaven, meant to be preserved on earth."

-*Anonymous*-

ADIEU

Adieu, my dear ones...
Time has flown like autumn leaves,
Five precious years, a treasure trove
of memories we've made....

Each and every moment with you
has been etched in my heart,
-A bittersweet symphony
that echoes forever!

As I bid adieu, my heart beats,
with mixed emotions,
Torn in between feelings of gratitude
and the aches of parting.

-Your love and affection,
 have been my guiding light,
Illuminating even the darkest
corners of my life!

Thank you for being my rock,
my support, and my haven.
I'll carry the memories of our togetherness,
Those tender moments, of joy,
tears, and triumphs...........
Very close to my heart.

Though we may be far apart,
know that you're forever in my thoughts,
And I pray, that our paths
will cross again soon.

The world may be vast,
but I believe it's the shared moments,
The laughter, and the memories
That matters, making it small and intimate.

---Forget me not, my dear ones,
for in the tapestry of life,
Our bond will remain forever intertwined.

Wishing you all the love, joy, and peace that
Life has to offer, as time passes by!!!

HOMEWARD BOUND

The take-off was smooth as the giant jumbo jet elevated up. The wheels were jarring as they soared high up into the sky. The aircraft was a twin engine Boeing 777-a marvel of engineering and avionics. It glided high up in the air transporting hundreds of passengers to their dream destinations. Comfortably seated in a cozy corner; I visualized myself flying on towards my colourful nest, bounded by walls of unbridled freedom. It's the colour of a safe warm place where someone takes you under the wing; feeds you with tasty meals, coos over you, hovers around you; providing all necessary comfort and protecting you from all evils.

This trip was meticulously planned. For months the excitement to go provides ample momentum to set the ball rolling. Hours and days are spent surfing the net to save each penny and bag the best ever deal so that the trip cost is optimized. Options are compromised and long waiting hours in unknown places are accepted as the mind is tuned on towards the journey home.

I have a label tagged to me-NRI. This is no ordinary label; it speaks a lot. To some I am blessed, while others see me as a bundle of wealth, some others perceive me as a traitor and hypocrite to my motherland while another just thinks I am a nomad who exists in a dream world. Each perception is focused on the perceivers' self-created imagination.

God has created the sky blue, plants green, soil brown and the ocean grey everywhere all around the globe; within this likeness coexists a great diversity of species. I am just a microcosm within this chromosphere. At times I ask the same question again and again curious of my self-identity and belongingness. People in the US think I'm too old fashioned, old-style, carrying around me the aura of culture and "Indianness" all around ... Yet, I stick to those basic morals, manners values and norms that have been programmed into my mental makeup since childhood. Instances like these have happened: my boss comes around my desk and lo-I instantly stand up with due reverence becoming a laughingstock of all. A friend nudges in and says-what's up -meticulously my eyes turn upward gazing at the ceiling, only after a pause I realize the significance. Harry sounds like Hari, Garie is my favourite Gouri and Grandier Lane is well remembered as Gandhi road -all messed up to make things familiar and less confusing. On the other hand, Indian people, consider me as a species from another world; because I'm too classy, chic and forward when it comes to US life. Suddenly I realize I am a total misfit it's like I have two sides of the coin. Juxtaposed within the clutches of two poles I remain standstill deciding my next course of action.

With time I have realized, the table has turned, the initial charm of meeting and greeting no more exists. The never-ending phone calls I make from abroad has no meaning, the gifts I carry for each and every one- picked up from the countless visit to stores: bought with saved clippings and coupons are not appreciated.

At times, it hurts as I sense the jealousy within others: elders always pamper me-when in sight, I am the preferred one. They do not realise how effective a therapy that much needed kindness has on my tired body and soul which is longing for that affection and warmth. bereft of parental love, security and attention I have learned to live in the present; every day is another day, a new beginning, hoping what is the best -that is yet to come.

Shopping in the local bazaars not only is a pleasure, but it is also nostalgic too. Eating out in local food stalls is not only fun and appetizing- but it also makes me, feel at home. Tagged as –"Firanghi", they laugh when I hunt for dustbins, napkins and toilet paper. Apparently, I do have a money tree in my backyard, thus obliged to squander at each and every opportunity.

On the contrary, it is indeed shocking: seeing my folks swaying under a storm of radical social change. Individuals all around have expectations of that glitter of a dollar which I have meticulously saved counting pennies, nickels and dimes bit by bit. Not to say that I am poor or selfish, no one will understand that not everyone in the US is a high paid worker. We as immigrants have our own initial struggles and be content mopping floors, vacuuming carpets, filling gas at the gas stations, baby sitting or standing in a store-these are chores which we would never think of doing back home.

A loom of uncertainty persists at the workplace as it is a common practise that the corporate world in a capitalist country adheres to the norm-hire and fire.

This sense of uncertainty kills us; we stand on our own having nothing concrete to fall back upon. I am what I am today or have because of my guts wherein I have flown offshore, faced a different world all together without any sort of support. I became frustrated as I spent countless days trying to make connections for a suitable job. Ironically, all surrounding doors shut like a dominoes game, one by one I realized, my doctoral qualification from India did not stand a chance in this land of opportunity.

Besides taking a hefty loan for furthering my education I have spent many sleepless nights struggling with the conscious decision of making this move. In a new country, when you try to talk to new people and hunt for a suitable job for yourself, despite having a work permit, no one really responds, and your decades of experience seems to have vanished.

Finding a job of your choice is not easy-hence one has to fit into any cuboid that provides you the space. In the workplace people many a times treat you as an intruder/threat to their own well-being and again a struggle for survival harbours. People of your own kind also behave in a different manner rootless as they are no one really welcomes or co-operates. Foreigners most often blame us for taking away their jobs and it is hard to prove one's integrity. The best part is-once accepted you become -The preferred ONE, moving up the ladder as lady luck smiles on your sense of perseverance and adaptability.

My old label as a snake charmer or naked fakir has changed to a better term -the smart techie. Nowadays, we have made our nation proud- All top Physicians in the US are Indians, NASA boasts about the majority of our bright Scientists. Extraordinary people like Pichai, Nooyi and Nadella, have topped the corporate world- a dream come true! Indian music is melody to the ears, spending money on an Indian movie is sometimes my only mode of relaxation. I would drive miles and miles going grocery shopping to buy that bitter gourd and white pumpkin- veggies I had once disliked. With time one realizes that the plain burfi jalebis and laddu's are far tastier than the readily available -cakes puddings and pies. Fast food is tempting, time has taught me to stay away from them due to health reasons, hence I have to imagine Mom and Dadima's kitchen and become an expert Indian chef within no time.

Life is not a bed of roses; it is not static. We all have to strive for the best. No place on earth is heaven one has to weigh the pros and cons of everything-looking at the positives. Consequently, we must all adapt to new situations. While we may not be comfortable with certain aspects of the Western culture, there are so many plus points. As with all cultures, there is a good, and a bad. The very best that I have learnt from this country is to be self-reliant and independent. Being independent doesn't necessarily mean loving less or not asking for help. It necessarily teaches you to letting people in and reaching out to others as per the circumstances.

This culture teaches you to strive for the best, be confident and enables you to be a fine, independent, young human being. We cannot control what life throws at us, but we can control our response to it. This response is our adaptability.

I have been fortunate to mingle with people of diverse backgrounds. With great enthusiasm I become a part of celebrations like Thanksgiving and Christmas as well as I enjoy Holi and Diwali. In a crowd – I would automatically gravitate around other Indians just because it's a natural talking point like, "where are you from in India? Do you have family there? Do you visit India often?" The queries are endless.

What is funny about India and "Indianness" is that sense of affinity-the love, at the very core-the Dil that remains Hindustani. India is ridiculous, dysfunctional the people amazing and wonderful, the pathways all entangled and shabby but in spite of all that-I jump at any chance to go.

Living close to your parents and relatives comes with its own share of obligations and family politics. It's amazing how much time is spent in India attending weddings, engagements, birthday parties and festivals. Probably that is the energy that keeps one vibrant and active. Lonely and cut off at times I yearn the company of my loved ones, holding on to past memories strong and firm.

Living in an alien soil for years, has made me stronger as I have learned the hard way to survive against all odds. Every storm that I have endured has taught me a lesson to grow and appreciate the present.

Success, for me has always been in providing a great quality of life for my family; seeing them reach their full potential. For sure, I have achieved the American Dream; it gives me immense pleasure and satisfaction to see each and every member of my family growing both at the social and professional level. I perceive my fulfilment of goals in their achievement.

Counting upon my blessings; I am privileged to breathe pure air, live in a neat and clean environment, eat fresh, healthy food and have access to state of the Art'-Medical facilities. As a common person, I enjoy a lifestyle worth to be proud off. Lucky, to have the best of both worlds-"! always like everything about being a debased desi". In updating my gratitude list, I am thankful for living in America.

-God Bless America!

...." Happiness is what we make of the circumstances and not what the surroundings have to offer."

-Anonymous-

MY ANGELS

Memories of people we knew and loved are all we have after they have departed. However, sometimes these memories help to fill in the emptiness those loved ones leave behind ages after they are gone. Even now, when I think of my aunt, Pani Mausi and Uncle, I treasure innumerable memories of them full of warmth, love and laughter. Recollecting those days of yester years, I had arrived in New Delhi, the capital city of India where things were completely different from my small sleepy town of Cuttack where I was born and brought up with lots of love and affection.

A shy bride, besides my husband whom I had barely known for a few days, my only other acquaintance in that big metro city was my cousin, Muni Nani. She lived at reasonably walking distance from my home with her in-laws...Pani Mausa and Mausi. Appreciative of the family connection, I had meticulously preserved her address and phone number.

Consequent upon my marriage, I had to leave my hometown and move with my husband to New Delhi. At the train station, it was stressful, as my mom kept relating sermons of do's and don'ts all in a row. I knew she was as anxious to let go her child as I was; equally excited and nervous to embark upon a new chapter of life, far away from home. Needless to say, this was my first train ride and the very first step in leaving the comfort of a protected, carefree childhood. Even as a college student I was always obedient and compliant. Hanging out with friends was not my cup of tea. My world revolved around the four corners of my home and family. Half listening to all the wisdom that Maa had given me these were the golden words, etched in my memory....." in case of any emergency you always have your Muni Nani close by, never be hesitant to ask for any help from her."

As expected, I got a warm welcome at my sister's place and became very much attached to her in-laws. Mausi would welcome me with a warm hug saying, 'Jhialo". Uncle would bring in a bowl filled with fruits, proudly narrating how much he cared for the local sellers as he picked his favorites. A loving home and family, I soon became one among them attached to the core.

My husband would go on business trips very often. I would take advantage of this opportunity by spending time with my cousin and her family. We cherished each other's company as we shared many things in common. Learning basic household skills and solving baby teething problems-Muninani was my "Google Guru".

Those were the golden days when modes of communication were not as they are now. We depended on local telephone lines with STD facilities. Akshay had gone to Vindyachal on an official trip, two days had passed, and I did not hear back from him. On the third day, I became anxious, worried and restless, I felt the need to go home. I could think of no one but my cousin who would help me in distress. Going alone to my cousin's place was not easy, obviously we did not have access to google maps. As per coincidence, I had observed a big house with a template "Nandas", located at the rear end of the road that would lead me to my desired destination.

Adding spice to my story, genuinely I thought it would be another Odia family whom I could conveniently knock, and they would help me find my cousin's home. My children would have had a hearty laugh, hearing such tales but that was the absolute truth. It was like locating a bestie's home by recognizing the familiar hairy bull that slept in the street crossing near the gas station adjacent to the famous, "Sahu tea and paan stall".

When I reached the big bungalow: to my utter disappointment I found out that the "Nandas", were a reputed business family-Punjabis' of South Delhi. The looks itself of the security guard in front of the house was indication enough for me to stay away from them.

Nevertheless, it gave me a lead, with great difficulty, I was fortunate enough to reach the Panis' residence. Interlocked tight within Pani Mausi's arms I kept crying relating in-between sobs as to how careless my husband was for not letting me know about his whereabouts. Crying out aloud: I demanded, "please book me a train ticket to Cuttack. I have to go back to my Papa's home," The child within me was aroused and I was determined to decide my course of action, as per the situation.

Comforted amidst caring souls, my brother-in-law made efforts to reach Akshay by contacting his colleagues in the office. Things worked out fine and very soon I was happy to hear Akshay's voice on the black cordless receiver at Pani Mausa's home. I was thankful, pacified and happy.

Years have passed since I have left New Delhi and rebuilt a new nest abroad. With time, things have taken a new twist and turn. Distance has never cut our ties rather it has strengthened the bond. I have always been in touch with my favorite cousin and her family. When I call up the number 26.....43, which is still fresh in my mind. I have never felt the need to write it down.

Remembering this episode, every time Mausa and Mausi would definitely wonder how I have managed to live so far in a foreign country?

-----It is all your blessings.....that has made me strong and adjust to life's different phases, I am still protected by my revered, Pani angels till date. Somewhere, for sure you are with me in some form. Furthermore, I know both of you are watching me from your heavenly abode and feeling proud of your child, who has matured over the years.

---"Maturity is the behavioral expression of emotional health and wisdom, it manifests with time, situations and circumstances."

-*Anonymous*-

WORDS OF WISDOM

"A child never tells a lie, I'm sure you believe it. You are a Psychologist and must know better than me", shouted Kiran as she ran down the stairs of their eighth-floor apartment.

Believe me, for God's sake today is Mahashivratri-an auspicious day of the Hindu calendar, I have done no harm to your child. I swear by God that I am innocent." Shruti kept pleading with folded hands.

Well! Innocence, sacrifice, sympathy, helpful attitude, fellow feeling all these emotions are perhaps things of the bygone days that have been deliberately erased from the modern-day dictionary as the present day's hectic life schedule is primarily governed by the basic dictum-TIME IS MONEY.

The words kept ringing in her mind, as the harsh confrontations echoed around her ears. Shruti, just could not believe that things would take such a nasty turn when her sole intention was to help a neighbor, derive psychological happiness in the company of a cute cuddly little girl and at the same time earn some extra money for the family.

It is always fate's will that takes the ultimate decision. Long lost from a warm, friendly and happy environment in which she was born and brought up today she feels dejected and helpless in an alien land

-a sapling uprooted from its native soil in search of some recognition and affinity-a basic self-esteem need as recognized by ' Maslow's theory of Psychological Needs.'

Things suddenly took a different turn in life, when Shruti's husband got an overseas appointment with a firm in the States. Yes, after all it was NEW YORK; the place which seems to be heaven - the city that never sleeps- controlling the economy of the whole corporate world. Who could deny such an offer! Yes, irresistible it seems. As family and friends came to know about it, eyes turned, ears whispered; people vied.

It hardly took minutes for her to think of resigning from the job from which she had derived an immense sense of satisfaction-a fact that she could at least use her talents in the right direction.

Family and friends had always made fun of her simplicity but at work she was a different entity altogether, smart, capable, efficient and willingly accomplishing any possible job that was assigned to her from time to time. The principal kept assuring her: "Shruti, you are a well-qualified competent and capable young lady- who knows you may be absorbed in a job of your choice earning more than your husband. A bright future awaits you... think positively, the sky ought to be your limit go ahead with your plans, take advantage of this golden opportunity-remember, opportunity comes only once. I am pretty sure success will be yours-our best wishes are always with you".

The calm and composed mind of Shruti also consoled her, alleviating the basic fears of jeopardizing a well-settled life. Go-ahead said the inner voice; for a woman my dear -family comes first-think of your husband's career prospects and the future of your kids after all, in their happiness lies yours.

Everything was final and soon the day dawned to bid farewell to family and friends as she boarded the international flight to join her husband and build up a new home with a renewed spirit of enthusiasm and vigor.

The initial euphoria was soon over; all the excitement and thrills that hung on for some time gave way to reality. Despite the beautiful surroundings of the suburb area of NEW YORK in which she lived and the comforts of modern day living that she had at her disposal, some sort of vacuum engulfed her mind, as the days flew past. Atul, a workaholic by nature, was engrossed in his job day in and day out. The kids who were old enough to look after themselves did no longer hanker for the company of their mother.

Yeah! She found herself to be a doormat with the burden of time hanging heavily on her shoulders. It is true, she was indeed the queen of her domain with none to question her actions, but nature perhaps had not made her that way to enjoy this life of sheer luxury.

Records behind her had always spoken about the true story of struggle that she had undertaken just to reveal to the world that she was indeed a gem hidden beneath the deep waters of the ocean. She wanted to prove that she was always an achiever despite all the odds that seemed to have come her way.

Today, all her efforts seem to have gone into thin air, as she found herself totally enclosed within the four walls of the home and hearth. The prime time of life, the most productive years when she could utilize her, brainpower seemed to be going down the drain. The truth lay in the fact that -without a job permit getting a job was not easy. It is rightly said -impossible is a word found in a fool's dictionary. Good friends and well-wishers always encouraged her- "Come on Shruti! Do not get disheartened keep applying, someday or the other victory will be yours". Yes, hope is the power that sustains life on the earth so there is no harm in trying and thus the days rolled by in the process of inquiry and investigations; hoping against hopes that something concrete might crop up someday or the other.

One fine morning, as she slept lazily reading a storybook on the couch, a familiar voice at the door beckoned her to get up and listen. Oh! She was, the known Indian aunty whom she had met the other day, she was wearing salwar kameez and spoke Hindi. " Come in aunty," she said as she lovingly pulled her into the living room. It was indeed nice to have the company of someone from your native land in a foreign country.

Aunty had brought along with her a little girl; she was her granddaughter, " Menaka" by name. Oh! What a lovely name that matches her looks so well. The delicate little girl was no less beautiful than 'Menaka", the celestial fairy of the puranas. Her mother perhaps did not have to think a second to give her such an apt name, I suppose, thought Shruti as she cuddled the tiny bundle into her arms giving her a big, big hug.

The grand old lady peered through her glasses and with a stern yet pleading voice said, "Shruti, you have to look after Menaka while her mother goes out to work for her babysitter has refused to take care of her anymore on grounds of ill health".

Shruti paused for a while and replied, "but I have

never looked after my own, as I have always been an outgoing lady leaving the aspect of childcare on other dependable people."

Menaka's granny assured her, "you do not have to worry much about Menaka as she is already toilet-trained and basically, she is a well-behaved darling. Moreover, you will be sitting at home, at least you will have someone to share your loneliness. Don't forget you shall be earning in dollars too. Remember, if you change the amount, it will be twice the salary that you were paid for the job that you did back home".

It wasn't a bad idea thought Shruti for her friend too was on the same boat and the dealing was between Indian families where she was doubly sure nothing wrong could ever happen. Moreover, they were bound to the same culture and differences if at all, could be sorted out with understanding.

Atul at first, was wary about the proposal "I 'am sure you will get into trouble, drop the idea - I earn enough for the family. Come' on learn to be satisfied with whatever you have. Isn't it a big risk that you are undertaking"?

Shruti laughed out his words ". Didn't I depend on others to take care of my kids when they were young-I feel there is no harm in this. I will be helping them in a way and at the same time have the satisfaction of earning some money on my own".

"Do whatever you like", was his ultimate and final word. A sense of victory for Shruti indeed! Because mostly his words ruled the home. This time it was hers and she felt so good about it.

Kiran was very happy; everything seemed to work

out so well because she lived in the flat downstairs. Shruti was well educated, and she was sure that her daughter would be in safe hands. "Is twenty-five dollars per day ok for you," she asked over the telephone.

Shruti replied, "I am so new to this place, and I know nothing about this I will ask my friend and tell you". Before she could say something, the money was pushed into her hands. Shruti did not mind it at all because Menaka proved to be a well-behaved child, and everything worked out fine.

Days, weeks and months passed by - 'MUNU', as she was fondly called, became the focus of attention in the Dutta family. Even Atul adored her, allowing her to sit on his head and shoulders. Shruti would anxiously wait to greet the girl every morning as her father came to drop her. The children who were normally noisy would come back from school hush hush tip toed-'Munu is asleep'.

Kiran soon realized and acknowledged the fact as to how much her daughter was pampered in the family where she spent most of the day. Shruti also never objected when on occasions Kiran had to leave Munu in their house and go out - for they had become family friends. One fine evening, Kiran related to Shruti, "Well, I have resigned from my job today and very soon I shall be joining another firm. Tell me if you are fed up with taking care of Menaka. Speak out your mind because this firm is far away from home and thus, Menaka will stay with you for an additional time of two hours. I do not mind paying you more for that, even I shall make up for the deficit if any, which is due to you till date. At least I should not be bothered about Menaka when I take up this new assignment."

Shruti laughed and promptly replied, "I have never said that I am ever tired of Munu, I shall definitely love to take care of her as long as I am at home. Regarding the money part I shall think about it and talk to you tomorrow".

"Money, money, money brighter than sunshine sweeter than honey". Who would not like to have more and more of it only a sadhu, saint, sanyasi will say no. Kiran has asked me to open my mouth so why shouldn't I thought, Shruti. It is utter foolishness to keep your mouth shut suggested other friends. "Now you are an American, you should learn not to allow others to take a ride on your back. Babysitters over here are paid on an hourly basis. Aren't you bound with that child for a pretty long period of time? She would never be able to get another babysitter at such a low price. Do you think you are going to get a gold medal from her for being the best babysitter in the world? Moreover, she is not a poor lady who needs help, you ought to open up and speak out your mind you should ask for more."

Yes, all her life till today she has always been exploited by others in some way or the other. This time she thought she would be wiser. However, Atul had given her the warning signal. "You never asked for the money that she is giving you now. If you open your mouth, you shall be losing your upper hand, remember if you demand expectations will arise and you shall be treated no less than a maid".

Ignoring his words, Shruti mustered up enough courage to speak out. "Kiran you have stayed in this country for long and you should have a better idea about the system of childcare. As I have gathered information from the people around here-the rate is much higher than what I receive so you have to decide and give me what I deserve." No sooner had the words finished from her mouth, Kiran immediately flared up speaking a lot defending her stance regarding the issue.

"Ok, Kiran, it is just my bad luck that I have always been exploited by others in whatever job I have been doing so far. Frankly speaking, I don't mind it 'MONEY' should never be a factor in destroying the lovely bond that we have developed with each other over the time period. We do not have our own kith and kin to help us over here, so what is the use of being friends if we do not share our burdens at times of need. Go ahead-forget about it." In a humble tone Shruti replied.

Over the weekend news reached Shruti's ears that Kiran was desperately looking for a babysitter. After listening to the whole story, well-wishers had advised her to stop having relations with that ungrateful lady thereby maintaining her own dignity and self-respect.

Once again, the inner voice within her prompted her to remain calm and composed. If Munu comes, she thought she would certainly welcome her with the same sense of affection that she had done before. The child should not be punished in any way because of the parent's arrogant behavior. She had in fact tried her very best to forget Kiran's diplomacy and patch up the hole.

Monday morning, it was Munu at the door. Her shrill voice could be heard "Soniadidi open the door". A voice that could melt a stone! Shruti immediately opened the door and greeted her father as usual. Munu, as it was a part of her daily routine, cried a bit as her father waved goodbye.

An emotionally chocked voice of Shruti blurted out, "It wasn't decent on Kiran's part to speak such harsh words to me. I still am unable to comprehend as to where I had gone wrong. She seems to be too smart it wasn't right on her part to behave in such a wild manner. Leaving little kids with others and going out to work is no joke. See, how much the child needs you".

Akhil, a gentleman by nature, just nodded his head and went off to duty. Things went on as usual, when the next day Menaka, while napping in the afternoon had spoiled the sofa. She had done this before also and each time Shruti had stripped off the sofa cover and had given it to Kiran for washing.

That day also she did the same thing. In the evening Kiran apologized to Shruti regarding her ill-behavior and once again brought in the subject of money to the forefront "Menka is fairly attached to your family", she said, " I do not want her to be separated from you people. It will become too much for her if she loses contact with you because she has yet to recover from the pain that she had to undergo of missing her Granny when she had to leave for Mumbai. We are prepared to pay you the money in any form that you demand as per your will- be it on an hourly or daily basis." Shruti at first evaded this issue after pausing for a while, in a very humble manner she said, " Give whatever you like I just cannot say anything," but on Kiran's insistence she said, "It's ok just give me thirty-five dollars per day that will suffice". Thus, the agreement was over.

As a part of his daily routine, Akhil always made it a point to ring up from office and talk to his daughter for some time. This time the tone was different, and he asked Shruti as to whether Menka was being taught every day with the books which they borrowed from the library for her.

Shruti at once recalled Atul's words; Teaching was her passion, and she loved to do it. All these years this was what she had been doing and how much she missed that part of life she only knows. Well, she never had taught little kids for this was a different skill altogether and she knew that she had no patience for that. She soon realized how much the giver values each and every penny that he has to part with. She was paid for the job, and he had all the rights to demand.

The sofa in Shruti's living room lay bare, she knew that both Kiran and Akhil were busy people and would get the time to wash the cover only during the weekend, so she did not ask for it. On the other hand, she covered it up with a bed sheet. She had the tendency to adjust to others, giving less priority to her own needs.

Next day, while Munu was busy eating noodles in front of the T.V. Shruti went to the kitchen to complete some of her cooking chores. After a while she came out of the kitchen and to her utter dismay, she found Munu completely engrossed in messing up the place gleefully pulling out bits of foam from the sofa.

She was busy with her job completely unaware of the consequences. A glance at the mess and a bewildered Shruti hit her own head with her fists and shouted, "Munu, see what you have done! A minute out of sight means you are up to some mischief or the other".

As was normal and obvious, the little girl started crying, as pearl-like tears rolled down her rosy cheeks. Shruti lost no time in trying to pacify her. The delicate child was like an ice doll ready to melt at the slightest spark. Anyway, experience had taught Shruti how to tackle the situation and she did it the same way as she had done before. Munu had her lunch and went off to sleep.

Kiran came in the evening to pick up her baby. As she closed the door Munu turned back, "goodbye, Aunty" she said.

Who knew that this would be the last day of Munu in her favorite aunt's house? As is usual for little kids to narrate the day's tale to their mother, Munu must have incoherently said something about the incident to her Mama. Kiran promptly rang up to know exactly what had happened and informed Shruti that Menka would not be coming to her house for a whole week as she was on leave.

Since it is winter break, the kids will be at home thought Shruti and she would not miss Munu much. She on the other hand, meticulously planned to finish all her outdoor errands over the time period.

One fine morning, a grim-faced Kiran came to Shruti's house and said, "Please hand over Menaka's personal belongings that are in your house as she is no longer going to come here. She herself says that she does not want to stay with you anymore."

Shruti could not believe her words, but after a second thought she asked her, "where will she stay while you are away from home." "I am going to leave my job", said Kiran, "it is just a matter of six months or so because very soon Menaka will be joining a Day school" replied Kiran with a burst of anger.

"Are you mad Kiran, please do not leave your job see how bad I feel sitting at home. I am willing to take care of Menka until you find an alternative. I am sure you will get one soon," said Shruti. "No, my daughter is my priority, she hates you and does not want to come to you anymore, "replied Kiran.

"Yes, it is the right and duty of every mother to look after her own baby, so do as you like", sadly uttered Shruti. Her brain could not analyze the complexities involved in the statement.

"Akhil has taken her today with him to his office just to heighten up her spirits. He will continue doing so till some arrangement is made. She has been traumatized, and you must know the reason. She fears you and shakes like a trembling leaf when we speak to her about you", Kiran abruptly answered.

Like a lunatic, Shruti ran into the bedroom, pulled out a small idol of the ALMIGHTY, clasped it tight in her hands and cried out. "Believe me ...." the distressed Shruti shrieked.

By the time she had returned back to the entrance of the flat where Kiran stood, she had already disappeared into the stairs.

The battle was over, and Kiran emerged as the ultimate winner!!!

After this sad incident: Shruti had to battle bouts of depression for several days and months at a stretch.

Realizing Shruti's agony, Atul patted her gently saying: "Once they're over let go of irritating things that happen. Dwelling on fights will only add to your annoyance. Remember, the truth is that - other people can ruin your moment, only you can ruin your day. It was just a bad dream!!! My dear, forget it".

--May his words of wisdom always reign in my home forever! With folded hands, this was Shruti's earnest prayer to the LORD.

WINGS OF FREEDOM

The inner voice within me spoke; I chose the path of freedom. The time is now, let go! Proving myself right used to be a major character flaw of mine. I had to face not one but many who needed justification, and gradually I realized it was futile. I stuck to my philosophy: "I don't care about what other people say about me. I know who I am, and I don't have to prove anything to anyone. "I identified my strengths and had to make a conscious effort to change my personality. Holding on to resentments was a burden and it made me all the more fragile. The realization dawned as I had to choose to hold on to either one pole from the East or the West. A single question got me started. Do you want to be right, or do you want peace? These magic words released me years ago and put me on the path of freedom.

-Time and tide wait for none. It is already four years that my ex-husband and I have been divorced. The boys have grown up and have left the nest to be on their own. In their late twenties, Ricky and Romy are fully aware of the situation and have accepted a new member into the family. As a mother I have never dishonored the image of their father and even from a distance the bonding has always been tight and healthy. This was something I appreciated and maintained.

Fate has its own plans; at a time, when we would have looked forward to seeing the kids spreading their branches, and bear fruits, things took an ugly turn. A part of the root got swayed, drifted, mingled finally getting entangled. He remarried, a young damsel 20yrs. younger.

He could not look at me the day when he confessed, he had a girlfriend. At first, I thought it was a joke and assumed this phase would pass. He was in India while I was busy looking after the kids in the US. He literally begged for freedom.

Leaving behind a cushy lifestyle and stable job back home, starting a new life from scratch was no joke. Like all immigrants we were dreamers and were determined to achieve the American Dream, giving a better future to our kids. Things were pretty stable at my end. His thoughts, words and actions clearly did not make any sense to me. I smiled with distrust and became sarcastic. Just as things were settling down. "You will ruin the boys' lives ", I had warned him.

Arnav was my first crush; we had dated for six long years and knew each other flesh and blood. Blessed as we were, we had the best education from premier institutions of the country and had landed up in prestigious jobs. He topped the Administrative Services while I had taken up a teaching job in a leading University. Amidst a big fat Indian wedding, we were pronounced as: Man and Wife. Witnessed by a large number of family, friends and well-wishers, we had taken the oath to remain faithful to each other not only in this but as per Hindu norms for seven more lives hereafter.

After a brief spell of Bollywood romance, we started a family with Ricky followed by Rommy, the love of our lives. As doting parents our life revolved around the little ones as we witnessed and enjoyed each and every step of their milestones: motor, language, social and emotional development. The kids had it all, as parents we were – picture perfect.

One fine evening, Amav came home with the good news that he was chosen as an expat representing the Indian Govt in a lucrative position at New York the financial hub of USA. Ricky and Rommy were excited to have a taste of the western world and looked forward to this change. Determined to achieve the best and make it happen we relocated to rebuild our home in the land of opportunities where lady luck (Statue of Liberty) stood strong and tall. promising a golden future to one and all.

Building a new home in an alien land was not an easy job, we stood by each other solid and strong, God's grace, the teething problems got sorted out and with time we gained foothold. Banking upon my Ph.D. I have been fortunate enough to get a teaching position in a post graduate State University which was pretty close to home. Both Ricky and Rommy loved the freedom of no boundaries school system that this nation had to offer. With a strong background in both Science and Mathematics, they skipped grades and were in most advanced courses, scoring a high percentile. The curriculum was flexible, satisfying and gave them a vision to a promising future. They dreamt of going to Ivy League schools and we were determined to provide them with the very best.

A carefree childhood with memorable prom days were over and the kids moved forward to college education. With the cost of higher education increasing we had started taking loans to make ends meet.

Like most Indian Americans, we led a comfortable life, living in a big house, driving luxury cars and planning the very best for our kids We were in debt, no worries, very much normal in a growing capitalist economy. I cherish those days; I was in the middle of a smooth sailing family boat.

Today, I look back, with no regrets, my loneliness gives me a chance to reflect on the past. I have always been a giver and that gives me immense satisfaction Arnav, was called back by the Govt of India to resume his high-profile job, he left us. I had pushed him to go, for I realized how much his career meant to him. with advancing age I thought, his cushy job with a Babu lifestyle of India would do him a lot better.

Moreover, I was capable and could handle things here in the US on my own. I presumed that day was not far, I would soon join him as and when my boys settled down in life. Living apart from each other had its own anomalies. A reversal of time added to the fuel. There is no doubt, of course: we missed each other. Priorities changed, I became more and more attached to my job, shouldering the full-blown responsibility of paying the bills, cooking, cleaning and slowly I fell into the trap of a robotic life pattern. Distance posed as an obstacle. Despite the modern means of communication, like WhatsApp and Facebook, we lacked the basics: human touch. I was too tired to respond and listen to my Man; he slowly drifted away from me.

The Bible says, God created Adam and Eve emerged from his rib meant to become a toy, dancing to his whims and fancies. Arnav became lonely and missed his family. I could sense his desperation; he had started taking more and more of those alcoholic drinks. I was far away and could not be of much help. My focus was on the kids. This situation created a perfect environment, "my Amav", slipped into the trap of a modern Eve. She was after his power and money. I was the giver, who gave away my husband to the wings of freedom.

"I should get going", I say. Yet, I have nowhere to be. I stand upright on a wrecked ship with strong sails as I look up to the Statue of Liberty. I have it all, my freedom. My job is my anchor; I pay my bills as they pile up at stipulated intervals. I have been a good mother and witnessed the joy of seeing my boys soaring high into the clouds with firm wings of their own.

Yet. I am in pain, but it's not sorrow, I feel it's a sense of relief and gratitude. I have done my best and banked on the love that is unconditional- expecting nothing in return. Our relationship came to an end because the partnership did not function properly, yet my love for Arnav remains deep within, forever.

-God bless America!

VOICE OF A MOTHER

At first, it all seemed so far away. Blissfully ignorant about the exact scenario, news all around, did focus on a strange virus spread in Wuhan, and I thanked heaven I am nowhere close, a big relief! That relief however was short lived, the virus had magic wings, and it was right here, close to home. Then COVID -19 hit, our town hard, things got very real, very quickly. Two physicians, who lived next door, with privileges at the local hospital were among those infected from that original pocket of cases.

Before we had time to think, the local hospital seemed flooded with a surge of new patients every day. The news was not something which we wanted to hear, it was nerve-wracking to hear about shortages in medical kits and the lack of facilities for the sick and ailing. Not to mention about the rising death cases. The best way to keep myself calm was to keep switching off that idiot box. "Fear", gripped the community. Spring was here, but people were hardly seen outdoors, the roads were deserted. As Covid cases swept across the world, it was sad to see and hear the heartbreaking stories of many. A basic struggle for survival. We silently prayed," our hearts are with one and all. "God's grace, this phase too shall pass". -God gives the strength to overcome!!!! At first it was someone, now it is within the family, scary scenario indeed. State orders called in for an official lockdown. Normal life patterns were disrupted everywhere, across the globe! Mother earth needed ultra - spiritual powers to heal. Almost a year has passed but for me it is like an unending day. I can feel the adrenaline pumping fast within me triggering my nerves and that anxiety practically never wears out. Oh no, I am not a frontline worker who has to go and face reality on the scene. I stay behind the curtain witnessing the agony. With folded hands, I plead for relief: I am a mother who has kids handling this project on the forefront.

At times, I would just sit back, and hope life would have been so much easier if they had chosen alternate career options. Anxious to the core, I became paranoid, paying extra attention to every small signal, be it a sneeze/cough or a slight whimper. Sooner or later, I realized, I was not alone facing this crisis; there were many more like me in my shoes. These past few months have been filled with heartaches for so many, and my heart goes out to those who have lost loved ones.

My daughters are my pride: Purbi is an Internal Medicine physician while Pari takes pride in looking after women health issues and delivering cute babies. Purbi and Pari, accomplished in each and every way, had families of their own with little kids.

I raised my girls to be strong, compassionate and serve humanity. Well, never in my wild dreams had I thought they would have to fight with strange armors on a battlefield. I felt helpless and prayed constantly. Geared up in their roles as care givers, they stepped up, conquered their fear, promising to do their very best. Working round the clock, all stressed up; we as parents could provide them with the safety net that they yearned for. This pandemic caused havoc to their work life, it was time for us to step in and help. Without second thoughts me and my husband volunteered to pitch in and intervene. Anubhav had his own health issues, yet he was willing to contribute. My hands were full, managing the situation with wobbly knees and a bad back. The responsibility of looking after their kids fell on me. My grandkids are my world, but to take full charge was a giant project. Both, Purbi and Pari had no other option.

The most difficult part for us was telling our children not to come home. This crisis has taught us all that health is a gift; we cannot take for granted. Safety was the priority, and we had to keep ourselves fit to take over this new responsibility. The little one, Lucy, was just 4 months old; she needed constant attention and care. Arjun was in his terrible twos', always on the move naughty to the core. Kajol, the five your old could understand a bit but she would often cry out loud swearing upon the Lord: "I would rather get sick, pop-up pills into my mouth, deal with the needle prick but would love to be with my Mamma ". Siddhant the eight your old, was my ultimate recluse, willingly he would help me out in every little chore that he could. He understood the gravity of the situation and had matured out of the blue.

Purbi's husband was stationed abroad in Dubai with an assignment and was stuck. The borders were closed and there was no way he could be with family. Pari had crazy working schedules, her husband had to look after his ailing mother who needed constant care as she was a dementia patient. It was not possible to get outside help during this critical phase, the little ones needed care and protection. We lived in the same neighborhood so for practical reasons it was better for the kids to stay with us. This served as the best logical solution as per circumstances.

I worried about my two angels, we had no time to

speak, a small message from them would elevate my spirits! Purbi worked heads on - directly on the Covid -19 unit. At times, she would burst out crying, no amount of face time with her little ones could give her solace. She would share with teary eyes; how difficult it was to work with patients who lay helpless awaiting the claws of death. Matters worsened when they left the world, without a close one beside their bed. Both physicians and nurses served as a point of comfort for patients who weren't able to be with their family members-whether that was about discussing last wishes, helping to Face Time, or simply holding hands. Purbi, often admitted to the fact that her medical training did give her some sense of preparedness to deal with this type of ordeal in day-to-day life; but dealing with this turmoil that Covid brought along at a massive scale gave her goose bumps and the residual stress was indeed tremendous!

Pari, my younger one, had accepted the fact that she had signed up on her way deep into a difficult path. She knew that this was her calling-the need of the hour, she did put up a brave front in spite of frightening situations. Her job as a ObGyn specialist had taught her to deal bravely with the pains/wails/the bleeding and the anxieties of her patients, on a regular basis. Her morale remained high throughout although the situation was still a nightmare. She made sure that the staff added informal smiling photos of themselves to the outside of their PPE, so that the patients- fellow front liners - could see who they were underneath their masks and shields. She tried to keep up her morale, taking advantage of all the multiple levels of support, including one-on-one and group counselling sessions that the hospital had to offer. One fine day, she taught me to download an app on the phone which would provide me sights and sounds of nature to keep control over my nervousness-the app- "Calm".

Both the sisters teamed up to help each other. They started taking all kinds of immunity booster drinks and pills. Right from tulsi/neem leaves to the humble ginger/ turmeric, everything was given due honor. Simple lemon and honey drinks replaced coke and coffee. Their medicine cabinet was well stocked with necessary vitamins and emergency drugs. They were well prepared to fight it out.

Under adverse situations, God gives one the strength to tide over. Both of us, as a couple, got a chance to re-experience our role as parents once again. We gained the strength to handle this adversity to the best possible advantage. Vedant and Shridhar often came to help us out in looking after the household chores. I became more adept at handling the little ones with great care and love. Our empty nest had become filled with cries, laughers, fights, yelling's and joy. My joints started cooperating, I had no time to complain about my bad back. As a best bet, it amazed me to see my fat melt away. As the days passed, at a very fast pace I learned my life had a new purpose and I was determined to live the fullest.

.......A weary mother can walk miles afar to put a smile on her child's face.

When Chris, our next-door neighbor developed sniffles shortness of breath and fatigue in mid - April we just hoped they were just symptoms of seasonal allergies. Within days, he developed a fever. Emma, my friend called up Purbi, "maybe your uncle has the virus," she recalls muttering incoherently. Protocols had to be followed, testing was not so rampant, the Department of Health had to be informed. Things went out of hand as with time, Chris's condition worsened. Purbi came to the rescue, with the help of the police an ambulance was summoned, and they got him admitted to the Emergency Department.

I felt the chill run down my spine, I bowed down and joined my hands tight, prayers and prayers. The medical team sprang into action. His oxygen levels were low, and he had to be hooked onto a ventilator. For seven days at a stretch, Chris remained in a medically induced coma in the hospital's intensive care unit. Every round Purbi would sit beside him and monitor the medication while transmitting healing vibes from the Lord. She made sure to call up Aunt Emma giving her updates about Chris's health condition.

Back home, an anxious Emma worried and waited while remaining isolated due to her own case of COVID-19. She would break down often and curse herself for not being more vigilant. Pari made sure that all our grocery shopping was done from time to time, while Shridhar did some outdoor chores. Emma's food basket was also neatly wrapped up for her, every single day. Emma kept blessing the girls for all the care. It was indeed a difficult time for everybody; we just learned to share our routine jobs. Despite the apprehension, both Emma and I learned to stay positive: our girls always reminded us that Chris was in the best of hands.

Gradually, Chris started responding to the care, his oxygenation and his breathing actions started improving. The Almighty had heard our prayers. With joys of tears both the girls shared the bliss about Chris's progress. Emma was ecstatic, she looked forward to the face time sessions with the love of her life. We were relieved. After spending a few more days at the Hospital, regaining his strength and vigor. Finally, the day arrived when he was well and discharged. As the ambulance pulled up at his home, family members greeted him with signs, balloons and flowers.

One fine morning I woke up to the sound of clapping's and honking as a crowd of neighbors had congregated on our front porch to acknowledge the services that our children have rendered to the local community. I cheered up, it was really awe-inspiring to have so many like-minded people to come over and treat us as, "celebrities".

This morning-the local TV channel showed: A confident Pari was chosen to be the first physician in our County, to be vaccinated. End of a dark era. Medical science has found the magic wand to drive away the devil and life could become normal soon. After two days, my brave girl Purbi, got the vaccination. Proudly she confessed on social media her poignant feelings; "for all of those patients that unfortunately didn't make it, all those patients still coming through the doors. We will fight this." Tough times give you a sea of hope for further progress.

Tears overflowing, I look back at my empty nest. Mission accomplished, today I wait in front of the portico to welcome my daughters with their families.

ROLE MODEL

I could feel the same pang of fear as I stepped in the footsteps of my son's home. For sure I was comparing my feelings to those days when I was young; a submissive bride at my in-laws' place. Cannot for sure forget that eerie feeling: yes, I was scared and uncomfortable.

Here I stand at another edge of life. A million queries ran through my nerve cells. What is my role and where do I place myself? My restless brain was just overactive!

- I had made up my mind to help and so the purpose was crystal clear.

Rhea and Vedant had recently bought a new condominium, and I was eager to see them settle down. Days have passed thirty - eight years from today I became a wife, a daughter-in-law, a mother and today I am a mother-in-law. My life has changed dramatically, I have seen myself swing; drastically opposite degrees in between two cultures and generations.

I did not know that one of the hardest transitions was going to be how to build a relationship with the wife of my son. The truth lies in the fact we both loved the same "Man". It is so natural, "Possessiveness", for sure - one should understand It takes time to immediately and readily share anything that you have held close to your heart all your life. As a mother I always believed that no one but only me could think and do best in the best interest of my child, I laughed loudly ...time for me to retire. This is the most common reason behind interference. I kept reminding myself not to unwind my past and had no warning for the road that lay before me.

In a dicey situation, the motherly love within me would overflow and outpour at times to do little favors for my child. The same things I had done for all those days since he was born. The list can be endless from cooking his favorite food..... doing his laundry or simply sitting beside him to listen to his frays while facing life outside the four walls of home. Insane for sure, I pinch myself every now and then; this helps me focus into reality. My baby has indeed grown up!

• A mother's job is to teach her children not to need her anymore. The hardest part of that is accepting success!

Born and brought up in the Indian soil as per the cultural trend of Ram Rajya my husband always was a devoted son for his parents. Many a times, I have been sidetracked and felt neglected. That was normal and I honestly accepted the view. Family was important and his happiness was respected. We as women were taught to be tolerant, silent and the goody - goody," sacrificing lady" type.

Nevertheless, my child grew up in the US. He witnessed a different culture in a digital era. Obviously, his thought patterns are westernized, modern and dissimilar. My joy knew no bounds when he introduced me to his fiancé. He believes in the dictum: A happy wife leads to a happy life! Once again, the mother within me, put in a big smile and proclaimed: "Be happy my child, I am proud of you and value your words, my daughter -in -law deserves your love, attention and care. My blessings are always with both of you. Make sure to be her- Champion; that she had dreamt of as a little girl."

They are busy nurses in a hospital and must put in long hours of duty. Proud of their professional achievement, it is nice to see them working shoulder to shoulder in the same institute. They met while studying in college and we are happy with the match.

A dear friend of mine had given me some valuable tips…...

-"Become an owl", she had advised:" Keep your eyes wide open and hoot all praises, that is the key for a proper bonding unto this fragile relationship".

With all optimistic thoughts in mind: I was determined to strengthen my bond. The welcome was warm and cordial, my fears vanished as I became more and more at ease. My mind is my master, and I discovered various ways and means to enslave it.

I was used to a fridge which was overfilled with groceries and the first shock I received was to encounter an empty refrigerator. On one shelf I found a gallon of milk, a few eggs and a loaf of bread. Another shelf had some fruit. I wondered what they ate. I started figuring out how to find the pots and pans in the kitchen. Not bad, I found some utensils inside the cupboard. Fortunately, I found some Indian grocery in the shelves too.

Thankfully the grocery store was at a walkable distance, I bought some veggies and cooked for the family. Both my children came back tired from work as I welcomed them to a nice homecooked meal. We sat together at the dining table and enjoyed the simple dinner.

No intrusions, I had promised myself, Rhea herself, revealed that their hospital did serve a nice lunch on the premises, and they had access to a healthy salad bar all around the clock. Other times they ordered food, with a click of a button. The modern market has so much to offer in the form of takeaways, uber-eats and drive ins. Things have changed for the better, a stressed lifestyle that our children lead, it is better to relax at home rather than waste time and energy in everyday cooking meals. I sure got the point straight.

The closets were full of clothes and several types of footwear crammed up to the brim. As busy professionals they had to dress up nicely to go and present themselves at work. The frequent seasonal changes demanded different types of jackets, so buying clothes as per style and season was an absolute necessity. No arguments: happy my children have a good dress sense.

No time to clean the home, it was messy with things lying here and there. My children never had the time to tidy up the house and keep their things in perfect order. Half their fights centered around digging for missing stuff each one yelling at another. Yet, the under the sink cabinet was filled with cleaning supplies of various kinds. My heart bled, one day I mustered up enough courage to explain that they needed to hire a cleaning lady, with basic cleaning done by a professional person rest of the work can be taken care of easily, Rhea, said she had no time for supervision. Time for me to take up the job, I volunteered to supervise and train the housekeeper so that in my absence she could continue doing her job with minimal supervision. I thanked heavens for solving another problem without much farce.

Working in the healthcare field has its own downturn, it is a commitment to unpredictable work schedules. The stress and anxiety level are high. Most of the time, I feel they are exhausted with less energy levels to cater to petty matters. I always have advised my kids to give more importance to their work, they deal with human lives, and it should be their top precedence.

Remembering, very well times have changed and so have the needs. It is hard to pinpoint where and how the pinch is felt. Giving each other space is the key to establishing a cordial relationship. I feel happy to see them doing things together. My son is no longer a baby; he is a family man and has numerous tasks on his agenda that must be fulfilled.

Here is the bottom line, as I see it. Mothers absolutely must understand that when a son marries, a new family has begun. That marriage is his NUMBER ONE priority. His loyalty and primary concern need to be with his wife and the family they create. This never means that the mother ceases to exist and must be cut out or shown no concern. It means that she has done her job in raising a man, and she needs to step away from any attempts to keep the mother-son relationship as a mother-buddy relationship. Her son is now a man and a husband. Failure to recognize this is the seed bed of most of the problems with daughters-in-law. Our Hindu scriptures also have mentioned: as and when the child attains adulthood a friendly bond with children is acceptable. This relationship thrives in the long run.

What happens is that when a mother lets go of her son in a healthy manner, a new type of relationship forms with both the mother and son. It's still a warm relationship, but it changes. It's like that old analogy puts it. If you hold a small bird tightly in your hand, you will crush it or injure it. If you hold it lightly while you care for it and feed it and then give it freedom, it will come back.

Moms who let go when the time comes go a long way in building trust with the daughter-in-law. It's about boundaries and respecting them. Proper boundaries are the starting point of all good relationships; I have found this to be true. In fact, one should always keep that in mind that it is impossible to literally start the next chapter of your life if you keep reading the last one over and over again.

Undoubtedly, it is a fact... the present generation is much smarter than us. They have access to modern technology to help them in many ways. Live, love and let live is the best way to balance and create healthy relationships. Helping my son sail his boat in a smooth manner is certainly more blissful than seeing him unhappy and wrecked.

The hard truth is....I have to leave this world sooner or later. Satisfaction in life is achieved by seeing the kids well settled and happy with their family. Love is not true, if it doesn't serve and sacrifice. Saints from time immemorial have always emphasized that the only formula for progressing in the path of Divine Love is to give and give without expecting anything in return.

I try my best to be a positive role model, cherishing the happiness of my children as they cross the innumerable milestones of life that they experience. Hurrah! This is indeed my victory. Silently I cherish the innumerable memories that unfold page by page. These countless reminiscences are absolutely mine- priceless, deeply embedded, with the passage of time.

-A mother's love for her child does not waver. Her care and concern are always there; it transcends the test of time. A tactful mother maintains the proper balance: this paves her path to the kingdom of GOD

This reminded me of a quote I really like by Warren Buffet:

----"It's a very strange thing about love- you can't get rid of it! If you try to give it out, you get more back. If you try to hang on to it, you lose it".

My loving, "Grannny"!

It is in the gentle breeze:
That I feel your presence
The leaves keep whispering
Your voice sounds clear,
"Keep trying, my dear
Success will be yours" ……
When I look up to see
The star-studded sky!
I know, the brightest one is you
Cause, it keeps blinking at me,
-Thou art in heaven.
Very close to God!
Blessing me with all," good luck"!
Your simple and selfless love.
Caring and understanding ways
It has given me the courage to move on
I appreciate the soothing comfort!
That has helped me stand strong.
---With every passing day
I feel your gentle touch,
An assurance and insurance of
True Love and well-being!
Unseen, unheard you keep
A watchful eye on me, shielding me,
From all evils, big and small

Your Philosophy of true dedication
Serving as a path to," Sure Success"
Has served as a key
Teaching me to appreciate
The beauty of life's
Fast revolving phases!
I realize it is only because of you
Today, I stand upright!
Thank you, my dear granny,
Thanks for all that you've
Done for me!!!

My World (Part One)

He was a very strong influence not on just the Indian community but everyone surrounding him. He was a visionary and the lead for me, a true -'Guru'. This man has given so many opportunities and created jobs for a vast amount of people throughout his career span of twenty-five years. Over the years he has witnessed the evolution of various technical procedures which have shaped the way he functions at the executive level. Fondly referred to as CM, he has donated his expertise and volunteered countless hours never forgetting where he came from.

When CM describes his early life, it seems extraordinary that he could emerge as a game-changer of any kind. He feels hugely grateful for many factors that have made him what he is today-the deep insight within, the craving for betterment, the blessings of his parents and above all – STARS! "Life has given me an opportunity I never could have dreamed of, coming from where I came from." He speaks. "I didn't come from the right school or fate did not bestow upon me that royal heritage".

-That of course, is an understatement.

CM's parents left school at a tender age and raised their six children under a thatched roof where survival depended on the farmland they possessed in their small ancestral village in a remote village of India. Once, I asked him about that strange wooden idol with glaring eyes placed on his office desk, he became enraged and very emotional. Proudly he claims that it is his Lord who gives him immense emotional strength, a nod to his childhood.

A typical day in his life begins with a prayer to this Lord of his land as he gets prepped up to handle the daily grind of routine tasks. As a kid, he was different with a weak body structure he was not fit enough to play in the sun and shade like the other kids. "I was pretty useless," he says." I was not good with my hands on a farm where everything was about your hands and body strength. I am fortunate to be the first in my family to step into a college."

With a twinkle in his eyes, you can always see the light of wisdom sparkle on his countenance. We worked in the same firm. As the pandemic raged all through the world, remote work became the norm. Our office became empty.CM was always there at his desk and I was there to assist him.

Even as he grew, he remained humble and grounded. One fine day he confided in me his journey: His tale, a story of triumph, hope and illusion. He wept as the tears trickled by and kept narrating his factual tale with a sigh of anguish!

-The child within him revolted, he always wanted to break the barriers that stifled him. He was a dreamer and dreamt big; constantly on the look for something more and the possibilities were limitless. His vision about the future was blurred, yet he was determined to fly into far-off lands, away from his modest yet secure nest.

His father very much wanted him to stay closer to home and motivated him to become a law enforcement Babu, of the village so that he would be proud of his son -working for the upliftment of his clan. Once again, the independent voice within him tried to break all barricades. With his mother's support and blessings, he got admitted to an Engineering College. A team of dedicated teachers supported his vision while he stayed away from the boys that just wasted their time and made merry. They of course were cushioned comfortably by their parents' wealth. Life in the city gave him additional opportunities to earn something extra by giving tuition to studious kids.

A brilliant mind, a scholar batch recipient, CM owes a lot to the scholarships that he received from time to time from the Indian Government for being a meticulous student. He solemnly admits, "my strongest memory growing up: I was always distinct from my peers. Four years of life in the dorm opened my eyes to a new world."

Those were the times when parents counted only male children as their heirs and women were just relegated to the household chores. His four sisters were destined to the home and hearth while the younger brother started helping his father with the farmlands. Armored with an engineering degree he became the "BABU.... Enlightened one," in the village. The campus selection in his college landed him a coveted job with one of the leading Multinational Companies in the capital i.e. New Delhi.

Everyone in his village cheered for their BABU, a pride for the family and community. Even after completing his Engineering degree, he had never gone too far away from home, and a train ride was something scary. He smiled and acknowledged the fact that he only had heard shady stories from his grandpa about his train journey from Lahore to India during the pre-independence era. His mother always encouraged him to achieve higher education. She did all the rituals and blessed him with a broad smile while bidding goodbye to her son. CM literally howled, as he remembered his foolish query to his friend Somnath, "how do I know that I have reached New Delhi station"?

Everything new, the metro capital offered a lot

for him to imbibe within him new traits to push himself forward. A decent salary gave him the motivation to work smart and handle new projects with diligence. Financially, he became strong, and it enhanced his confidence, he became more confident besides being independent. Most of his earnings he used to send it to his father, God's grace the family started enjoying a better life. One by one the sisters got married and he could see the pride and satisfaction in his parents' eyes. Bholu, his younger brother also found a partner for himself. Bholu could now hire help: money power spoke!

His parents felt gratified and entitled that their son could support them. Their thatched roof was replaced and with pride, they boasted of a new English style privy. Awesome! The villagers flocked to come and have a look at it. His Mom boasted about her new gas stove, refrigerator and TV. Evenings were chaos, neighbors from far and near came to watch their new in- home theatre. It was a victory for CM he rejoiced," I gave myself a thumbs up and worked harder touring all over the country, I was determined to make more money. I played with my cards and almost always became the winner."

Work kept him busy and motivated. During periodical holidays he would go back to his village, spending time with his siblings and their children. This short break was a stress buster for him. In his mind's eye, he still remembers packing presents for each one of them and the joy he felt within when he saw the gleam in the recipient's eye, it was remarkable!

His, Mom like any other parent, wanted him to get married and settle down. Afterall; relationships are a part of your life. Your life is not a part of your relationships. The fact was, as he grew older it became harder for him to make a decision: He looked for something more......She had to fit in perfect, everything uncomplicated! No two-faced personality... no hidden messages in between the line... no fake friends and no fake laughs... unedited photos and lots of laughter. She was supposed to blend in fine, ensuring the fact that sharing and caring for the extended family would never be a problem. His dream girl was nowhere in sight, and he just did not want to compromise.

Within a span of 4 months, one after the other his parents left for their heavenly abode. Each time he was at the graveside he could feel a sense of fulfillment; the tears and sadness were literally more of a fluid connection of eternal love. His grief served as a sacred pathway into a deeper connection within. Even today, he says he can visualize them sitting on either side of his shoulders: his guiding light. With the intensity of emotions surrounding loss, years rolled by and he became a forced - **Bachelor.**

In the absence of parents, basic connection with the ancestral home gradually diminished. A strong breadwinner of the family kept sending money home for various exigencies like medical expenses and education costs of the children.

Blame it on his stars, he was chosen for an assignment in the USA. It was hard to say no; he had never dreamt of foreign shores but yes it was tempting. Money is definitely not the primary reason to sacrifice all that intangible happiness in life of leaving your own soil. It's the level of exposure in a foreign country and the career opportunities that help move forward with one's goals and of course, he looked forward to giving himself a trial to a comfortable future.

In his very own style, he sniggers, "I describe myself as a risk taker with a basic motto; Luck favors the BOLD!

Leaving behind a cushy job, with a meager amount of dollars in my pocket I landed in the land of opportunities …New York. Hey, I said to myself, same old wine in a new bottle that's nothing great as I had dreamt. I could see them all: glittering neon lights, the big bold boards, and the skyscrapers except that the people were different. It was hard for me to understand their accent. Once again in life, I could feel the touch of poverty, for sure I was a poor man striving to have a foothold in the richest economy of the world. Determined, with an incandescent presence of mind with unflinching courage and guts, my struggle continued. Every dollar was converted into INR with a low profile and simple lifestyle I tried to blend myself into the new setup."

Americans failed to address him properly. He laughed, "my name itself became a roadblock, fondly named by my uncle - Chinmayananda, was difficult to pronounce. "I preferred it to be left only to the initials, but with time I became the popular CM in my workplace. In a progressive country like USA, it was not easy for me to propel myself in rough waters as ethnicity race and color all factors played a subtle role in the form of discrimination and alienation."

Recalling those initial days of struggle gives him goose bumps. From once again going back to school, getting an American degree and passing the licensing exam everything was tough. With the grace of the Almighty, as time flew, he could perceive a light at the end of the tunnel. Along with his own financial crunch, he had to oblige and undertake the burden of financial responsibility for his family that he had left behind. The fact was that no one back home was earning decent money.

At a personal level, CM vented out his anger and feelings:

"Teach a man to fish, and you feed him for life

Buy and give him fish for lunch and you feed him all your lifetime..........."

For money sent home to have life-changing impact, that money has to be invested in the education and skill development of family members so all can stand on their own feet instead of becoming a lifelong liability. The family has to be willing to change their life with sincere effort.

Unfortunately, many people in India think that people abroad pick money from trees rather than actually earn them. So, they make unreasonable demands and have unrealistic expectations of financial aid. Such people just want to enjoy handouts and have absolutely no intention of ever becoming financially self-sufficient. Needless to say, even 20 yrs. after continuously being supported, their quality of life remains as it was on day one. If you ask anybody from a developing country, there is this belief that you are a personal piggy bank. After all, you live in America. You make tons of dollars a year - that means you are rich. Therefore, you will have to weather all the requests to help your relatives back home. Somebody lost their job. Somebody wants to go to college. Another one is sick with mounting medical expenses: the list is endless. Here comes the request and the guilt trip to send them money.

True, CM did make a nice living in the US, but he also lives in Manhattan, one of the most expensive areas of the US and even the world. Nothing here in the US is cheap, leave alone the education costs, housing and to add up the Government sucks up a chunk amount of the salary in the name of taxes.

His attachment to his nieces and nephews was pure love and he always wanted to help so he kept stretching his budget. He knew very well refusal comes with a price:

the relationship with those relatives becomes strained and tense after such un-honored requests, after all, it is up to family to help.

His recent trip to his village gave him an insight into the fact that his siblings had become old and relegated to the background. The present generation of grown-up kids was extra smart they just looked for a ladder to climb up. Thankless, without any focus to look into the future they just knew to enjoy life at the poor guy's expense. With no kith and kin of his own blood reality dawned upon him. One fine evening as he walked past the street of crowded New York City the Wall Street BULL mocked at him. He got reminded of so many Bull fights that he used to witness on the village streets. That question immediately popped on .... "Who am I and what is my destination?" Sleep had eluded him and even the recently hyped guaranteed and highly priced" Sleep Mattress", failed to give him a good night's rest. Grumpy and tired he could feel the absence of that bull within him. He was no longer the go-getter; he realized the need to be anchored. Rising up the corporate ladder, he had become a leader, yet he lacked happiness. Living a life of loneliness, he started yearning for companionship, someone with whom he could share and care. He looked back to his savings and for sure he had almost nothing to fall back upon. Living at an old age home alone in US meant possessing a lot of wealth which of course he lacked. Like a bird, he had the urge to return to his nest i.e. his village.

His decision was firm, that night he could not sleep, the euphoria of returning home stole away his sleep. After all every evening a bird always looks forward to flying back to his nest, he made up his mind to spend the rest of his evening years with those whom he loved and for sure have missed them a lot. Reality dawned upon him; one by one they explained: "It would be hard for you to stay over here. Staying, so long in a cold climate it would be harsh to adjust here in the heat. You will miss your friends and the work atmosphere. Our place is still not tech-savvy like the Western world. Healthcare is not advanced here. The basic infrastructure is weak." This list was endless.

These negative comments were enough; his hopes were shattered. Nobody wanted to care for an old dog, all they wanted was the money that he would remit from time to time. He had to admit that this refusal to accept reality is emotionally draining, especially when you see that your country of birth is becoming nothing short of a humanitarian catastrophe.

So, think twice when you say, "I really want to live in the good old days." Think about what it really means. No one seriously wants to go back into a penniless state. It is the little emotions attached to familiar surroundings that beckon us. The shade of that familiar banyan tree, the gurgling brook that goes on forever, the green farmlands, my very own familiar hilltop, the path all along the riverbanks, that chaotic little bazaar and everything else so close to one's heart. Tired of having simple food, like salad soups and sandwiches he yearned for the elaborate and ethnic Indian cuisine that he used to get in his village.

Today, he sits silently in the corner of his room thinking about the future. He burst out loud," I miss the times when I had no idea about my future. When I see a couple walking hand in hand, I feel sorry. Well, it's okay, I don't have any stories left for this category. I am simply worthless!!"

Long story short, he added," I miss being a child. I miss not wearing business attire. I miss being myself. Thank you, dear world for all things bright and beautiful!"

I listened with awe to all that he said. Illogical for sure all messed up, I could decipher CM's longing to be loved and wanted. I hugged him tight; assuring him everything should be ok. Yet, knowing not in which and what way I could support!!!

----"The pain of not having connection is one of the only things that can burn deep enough to make us get out of our own way in finding love."

-*Anonymous*-

My World Changed (Part Two)

"I may need your help sometime today, will call u as per the need." I received this message from CM. It was vague, and I did not think much about it. That day he was not in the office, and it was unusual, but I just took it easy. I missed his presence, engrossed in my work I did not realize how fast time had slipped by. Evening at around 5 pm a call from the local hospital broke the news.

CM was hospitalized and an emergency angioplasty was inevitable. They needed me to cosign the papers and my presence beside the patient was desired. Without any delay, I was at his bedside as the white-winged angels took charge of the situation. We both prayed and wished for the best.

In tense times, CM had only me to bank upon. My family understood my priorities, and I stayed composed in the visitor's room. Spending long hrs. in an emergency unit was a daunting affair. Time just seemed to stand still, as I witnessed the sight of grieving families. Thankfully, my profession was not related in any way to this kind of humanitarian stress.

An unfamiliar ringtone amazed me; on second thoughts I answered it. The call was from CM's nephew from India, probably he had already given them the news about the impending procedure. We exchanged a few words, promising each other everything should be fine.

Finally, the doctor revealed, everything went well,

CM was shifted to the recovery room. On my way to the hospital, I grabbed CM's deity with me. I clutched it tight, the Lord is with us, this made his eyes gleam, and he reciprocated, with a pale yet pleasant look.

For some unusual gifts in life, unboxing is not fun. This was an inherited gift, packed and kept secret deep inside his chromosome. His mother had Ischemia and was always under regular treatment. His other siblings were diabetic and everyone in their family very well knew about their raised blood pressure level.

"I eat my medicines daily; I have no complaints,' he would say. He enjoyed working and had never thought about health hazards brewing up with age.

While conducting scheduled meetings from all over the world and talking to his clients in the office, nothing' happened. It was on his way back home climbing the little hillock he could feel that sensation. The tingling pain was so intense, he could not proceed any further. He sat down for a while till the pain subsided. He drank two sips of water from the water bottle that he always carried- Indeed, that saved him!

He admitted it was the first time in his life he felt scared of his lonely existence. Somehow, he reached home and collapsed on his bed. Fortunately, he woke up, as he dialed 911 seeking immediate medical help. Within no time the ambulance arrived with a team of caring professionals. Narrating the scene, he vividly recollects. It was a host of men God sent; they took charge of the situation." God bless America," he kept murmuring. In his mind's eye, he visualized all the Hindu Gods; they were all there to help.

'So how do you feel?' I asked, as I went to meet him when he was his normal self, resting cozily in his recovery room. "I feel GOD has been kind, I am glad to be alive," he said with a broad smile on his face. It was that smile of triumph, something very much akin to what I would perceive as the same occasion when we achieved success in bidding huge contracts for official matters.

He showed me the small mm. size swelling where the catheter had gone in. A small blister. His fair skin looked pale." It is nothing, it will heal in no time," I assured him.

We video-conferenced with his family in India. I turned to the family and said in a hushed tone, 'we are so lucky to get him back. I actually thought we'd lost him; 'God is great'. A personality with a magnanimous heart, he requested his nephew to feed a host of poor people in his village, as a symbol of gratitude.

Next morning before I could ask him, he jumped up and announced, "I am absolutely fine; ready to go home today." The doctors were ready to discharge him; I had already made arrangements for Emily, a trained home health aide who could cook and take care of him while recovering at home.

Diseases, however severe they are, when silent, don't bother a person. The side effects of a procedure, however minor or trivial it is, somewhat bother him; he attributes it to deficiency of skill and negligence of care; more because he feels that he has paid for the treatment. CM realized he needed help and care. Thanking the Lord: Life-threatening it was- indeed, a major problem was solved!

Apart from some inconsequential health checkups, life soon became normal for CM except that Emily had become an integral part of his lonely existence. Her presence definitely helped and made a difference. After years, he could feel the care and love of another individual and it worked like magic. He was happy and his happiness was apparent in his overall behavior pattern.

It's said that love is tested in crisis or in great happiness (strangely) but the most testing time of all for love is when there is - literally - nothing untoward happening. She cared and he responded to her loving actions. All these years, he has been a lone wolf, engrossed in his work. The pandemic added to the woes wherein human interaction became dim and life became, all the more... mundane.

He admits he looked forward to Emily's daily visits, he could feel the spark within. He confided in me, and I understood his predicament. True love should never be about investment; it is not a game. It is the greatest feeling that you can have in your life, so it is a good move to take risks in the name of love, even when you are uncertain about the outcome. Afterall, Love created us. So, it was my direction to him, "always express your feeling, because they matter. Be honest with other people, be honest with yourself," I suggested.

--- Feelings communicate much better than words do. My mantra worked, a beaming CM happily announced his love for Emily and the rest of the story just became history. The universal reaction was not favorable, back home his relatives were dead against such a relationship. They laughed and uttered nasty words about Emily who was referred to as a "fair-skinned trapper", she was the - seducer.

CM a grown adult, took his own decision. With a small gathering of friends, they got married. I could perceive the change in him, after years it was nice to see him going home on time. There was a purpose for him to go home now. Home-cooked meals and the magic touch of a caring wife worked wonders! The happiness glowed on his countenance, and it overflowed onto each and every aspect of his personality.

Over the years, they adopted two beautiful kids into their family. CM a scholar himself, took extra pain to look after their scholarly pursuits. It was interesting, he kept taking time off to be a part of the family.

Time for CM to retire, the office was all decked up to give him a fond farewell. I sat down with him for a short chat and asked him about his future plans. Immediately he cooed…... "God bless America"!

He added this country had given him an opportunity to be self-determining, rise and shine. It is not that he had forgotten his village, and all the good things associated with his motherland. The truth remained his contacts and resources over there were limited. Advanced age would give rise to more health problems, and it is a fact, undoubtedly the reality remains that the American healthcare system is incomparable to any other place on earth. His only resource with him was his hard-earned money and the God-given family which he had to lean on.

Every American citizen enjoys the much-needed independence that each and every individual aspires to achieve in order to survive. One has the free will to live one's own life the way he/she wishes. There is no interference at any level be it your work or family. To be perfectly frank, age 18 really is the age when a person in the USA can be truly and lawfully 'independent' of his/her parents or legal guardian in terms of physical movements, ownership of assets or possessions, etc. Without the shackles of weird norms taboos and unnecessary do's and don'ts this soil of America nurtured CM's spirit to soar high up in the corporate world.

Ishi and Ivan were growing up and they needed guidance and support. Emily, his loving wife was a God-given companion. His priorities had changed; he had already made plans to become a consultant in the firm thus actively involving himself in his work that he loved to immerse himself in for all these years.

Fumbling, with a choked tone he whispered into my ear, "this money which I have earned all my life long in this foreign land, is all that I have, my kith and kin always had an eye on this big resource of mine. In my state of helplessness and disability, I shall be always blackmailed for my money. Ultimately, I would be robbed, which is my absolute fear." There was indeed no scope to look back."

Retirement is delightful for most largely because it lets you make decisions based on something other than where you can draw a paycheck. But it is silly to expect a stranger to tell you where you will be the happiest and secure in every dimension. Life is more complicated than that, situations differ, and each one has his own views as per the circumstances.

He grabbed his Jagannath, and coolly nodded, "the Lord is with me, I came from nothing, His grace I am indeed blessed" ....Happy, Chinmayananda had made a firm pronouncement." The road was difficult, yet I am contented; that I had made my own way all through", he proudly proclaimed.

He had the opportunity to rise, soar and shine. His world had indeed changed for the better. The truth is: WE all deserve to be loved and live our own kind of happily ever after life.

----"Happy lives don't just happen but something that we have to decide that we want and actively pursue"!

-Anonymous-

SMASHED BARRIER

The ringtone stopped. I could hear his voice clear and profound," Sorry, I am not able to answer your call right now, please leave me a message and I will get back to you asap." I wondered, paused, and gave his words a thought.....for sure I could hear him well. Those words kept resonating: I felt dizzy.

My son did tell me, "MAA I have tons of jobs on my agenda! I am just being realistic: remember to let me know at least 24 hrs. in advance when you need my help." Oh boy! This was not a normal chore, like getting the Christmas decorations from the attic; or fighting with the credit card company for a fake bill. This was a genuine call, and I needed his presence. I was at my wit's end till I climbed up the stairs to bank upon Edwina, my neighbor.

It was a cold, blustery winter evening in January, '2020. This week the weather had been miserable, and we could hardly sneak out. Mother Nature had dumped loads and heaps of snow. Mahesh had finished his supper, and I could hear a sudden thud on the floor. The glass tumbler in his hand had broken and a piece had cut a vein in his right hand. I was horrified to see him bleed so fast. He was on blood thinners. Within no time, I ran to call Edwina my neighbor who worked as a nurse at a local hospital. Luckily, her son was with her and both of them acted fast to take care of the situation. With advanced age, for sure we needed support and help. This was an emergency, yet I could not contact my son who lived half a mile away from us. Mahesh was already taken to the emergency room; the cut was deep, and the bleeding was profuse.

There are so many times when we need our children more than they need us. They have no clue what they indeed, do for our souls! I cursed myself, as I cried, "inconsolably". Have I failed in my duty as a "mother"? My baby, my only child, always has been the apple of my eye. A slight whimper or cry would alert me to pay attention to his childhood nuances. The list is endless- all that the mother can do for her baby.

I named him Neil, for me he was Lord Krishna reborn, the pregnancy was not an easy one and he was the eighth one my - marvel boy! As parents, we doted on him and gave him the very best of everything. Mahesh worked two jobs to make ends meet, while I stayed home to take care of him. So many times, I keep wondering whether that was a fair enough decision for me to give up my career and raise my child. My options were limited, this child was God sent, and my priorities were all set around him.

The same child who would not let me out of sight for a minute is so busy that he is not available for us in times of exigency. A deep insight within pointed a finger toward me. Oh! Yes, it was our fault. Unconsciously our love for our only child was so intense that we fell into the trap of being overprotective and controlling. Our intentions for our child were good, but as he grew up, he wanted to be carefree and independent like his peers. All he wanted was to spread his wings and find his own identity. As soon as he found a job to sustain himself, he moved out of our home and wanted to stay in a rented place of his own will. I made sure he lived close enough. This ensured we could meet often and be available in times of need.

It broke my heart when he packed his stuff and left. My little boy had grown up; he was mature and was craving for freedom, Consciously, he had created a barrier between us and himself that would free him from our nagging interference.

With the advent of the digital world, our kids are exposed to an array of possibilities within the maze of accomplishments and failures. Decision-making is a strategy that is best acquired while swimming in troubled waters. A lion kept in a cage would never learn to hunt for his own food. The liberty and freedom to be on your own as an adult teaches a young mind to steer his own boat. This experience is a must; it not only liberates but also empowers a person to be a strong individual.

I realized: Part of growing up is learning how to recover from mistakes or failures. It is like the way the mother Giraffe teaches her baby to stand upright. By being overprotective children don't experience that important learning curve that will take them to solve more adult problems when they get older. I acknowledge the fact that this crucial learning should have started for Neil at the age of 22 and not at 42, This way he would learn to act according to his own will rather than becoming a people pleaser.

With all good intentions, we try to protect our children from anything bad that might happen. This anxiety overflows to the extent that we dictate and monitor the actions of our adult kids, smothering their ability to stand up for themselves. In extreme cases, this discord leads to friction breaking the lovely bond that has taken years to thrive.

God had taken care of the "crisis", I thanked Edwina for her timely care and help. Mahesh came back from the urgent care unit with a big bandage on his wrist. The storm had passed, like every other day the sun rose, to a new beginning.

Early morning, Neil responded to my message. Sadly, I told him about yesterday night's mishappening. Within no time Neil, my pride, was at our door. He felt bad and cursed himself for not being able to help us in time.

I realized, he no longer needed any advice.......all he needed was support and compassion. I knew The Lord would guide his path to take the right decisions all along. Happy that he has learned to find happiness on his own; with a spirit of freedom.

The gem of a son was learning to be brave and independent; we assured him that we would always be there with him as strong pillars of support in times of need. Care and compassion for each other are properly measured when there is true "love". Thus, the barrier in between was smashed with a big, "hug".

Mahesh stood up and greeted his son with a big smile.

---"Family is where life begins and mutual love for each other never has an ending!"

-Anonymous-

MESSAGE FOR MY LOVING DAUGHTER

---Message for my ………. loving daughter Supriya

Befitting the very meaning of her name….. "Supriya," she is loved by everyone be it young or old, she makes friends easily, that's her specialty!

To be very specific:

Mo jhia paree

Kiye heba

Udee jauthiule udanta chadhei

Dharee anee kiye deba……

This means: Supriya is unique, no one can be like my baby. She is capable of catching hold of a flying bird high up in the sky, it implies she is a high achiever, competent enough to conquer the impossible!

Meri pyaree gudiya Supriya

Nanhi munni si Supriya

Asman ki paree Supriya

Meri ankhon ka tara, meri Supriya……….

She makes us all proud!

How time flies…… you are a big girl now! I'm so happy for you that you have found the special one with whom you will set your dream home.

When I first met Sachit, I could feel the vibe of a virtuous person, an instant liking, I may be a little more than biased, but I am sure I am not alone when I say that our [groom] is a person who is kind and generous. Soft, spoken and gentle, he certainly has a heart of gold.

Hats off to his parents, who have raised him in a loving home for making him what he is today.

..........Sachit and Supriya..... for sure you are sacha-super match...God's grace.

My earnest advice to the two of you is: as you walk through this life, cling on to one another through the storms and enjoy every rainbow hand in hand. Never go to bed angry. Sounds like a cliché, but it's true. Learn to respect each other despite differences. Remember, my dear, your love is forever and a lifetime. Share every fear, every vision, every milestone together. I wish that every single dream you have comes true for "you".

You have a wonderful sister-in -law and brother - who are there around you, they are there for you on your journey, and you have learnt how to make it a teamwork always- not alone- never.

You are lucky to be in this country, where you have beautiful surroundings, a congenial environment and most important are the friends, colleagues and relatives that you have in abundance. Seek their opinion, if you have an unresolved puzzle, you have learnt enough out of your workplace, how to bundle advice from all, but finally take your own decision and own it. This will set your spirit free!

Congratulations! Both of you have found your true love. May this love grow stronger and deeper with each passing day. Complement each other and multiply your strengths!

As parents, we will always remain as supporting pillars beside you for all times to come......

March on......

March forward together........ fulfill your goals and you will be able to bask upon your achievements. God bless you!!!!!

-------Trying to cope up with the emptiness that u have left behind. Values in life are to be instilled, nurtured and protected.

With lots of love and affection,

"Maa"

DAD-MY HERO!

The summon was sudden, he had to leave for his final journey. All human efforts to save him ended in vain. I stood helpless before; I could embark on the reality! I felt numb, grief-stricken, cheated, and lost all faith in the Almighty. A staunch believer of Maa Kali; be it rain or shine; there was not a single day that he would not go to the temple. He gained immense strength from the Goddess to fulfill his worldly duties. Unbelievable, where was the Goddess? Why couldn't she protect him? Stormed with waves of ifs and buts I lost all hope in every natural and supernatural power. My eyes had no tears, I realized I had to face the status quo. Left in the dark, I had no other option but to accept reality and be strong.

My father was a highly successful attorney, often featured in various media outlets and widely recognized as a public figure. His success essentially was attributed to his exceptional insight, with superb analytical skills. He won numerous cases that others deemed impossible, earning him the nicknames "expert" and "genius" among his contemporaries. Many in the legal profession considered him a mentor, from whom they learned valuable lessons. Given his remarkable abilities, it's no surprise that he was affluent. His beautiful dream home a lovely bungalow remains, a testimony of his rich taste and elegant lifestyle.

Coming from a typical rural background with humble

beginnings, he had a hard life to begin with. Tracing back to the times of the pre-independence era in India as per the social norm families were large. Dad was the fifth kid of his parents, Unfortunately, the older ones did not survive, so as per the ethics in those days his parents gave him away to a beggar. This social act ensured the parents that this child would live and so they named him, "Bhikari Charan", which in our mother tongue means - Beggar.

Retrospective, one thinks.... Which parent in the perfect sense would name a child as Beggar? Maa had mentioned that, when she had first heard the name, she disliked it. My grandfather had assured her that he was the perfect candidate. His middle name was Charan which means feet. Grandpa understood that he could foresee a bright future in his chosen son-in-law and stressed that one day he would shine, and beggars would come and fall on his feet. Fondly he was called, "Bhiku".

As a staunch believer of, "Maa Kali;" he justified his name saying that he would always beg for wisdom, health, wealth and direction only from the divine 'Lord, "and none other. Growing up he lost his mother at a very young age and had to take care of three other siblings as well as his father who was a priest in the local Shiva temple. In school, Bhiku, became the favorite of his teachers. Obedient and modest he excelled in his studies and earned the attention of not only his teachers but also the executive head of the village. Adopted as a son, the Zamindar (God father) paid all his educational expenses and encouraged him to pursue further studies. With limited resources, he strived hard to study and encouraged his siblings to attain educational degrees. He had repeatedly expressed, that he would boldly walk for miles and miles from his village to Cuttack. The old city, "Cuttack" of Odisha had adequate facilities for adding more and more essence to his thirst for knowledge.

With the help of his maternal uncle who owned a food stall in Cuttack, he gained his foothold in Cuttack. Doing petty jobs here and there he passed High School and joined a college to pursue higher education. After graduation he did get a government job. This job provided him his basic daily requirements while he studied hard to become a student in the local, "Madhusudan Law College". Daytime he used to work while at night he used to attend the Law College. As he gained more and more confidence within him, he brought his siblings and stayed in a dingy dorm, making sure that each family member had enough to eat and survive. I have heard he used to study under the streetlight as he had no access to electric supplies at home.

During that period, the Odisha Judiciary system was primarily dominated by highly reputed and intelligent lawyers who were mostly migrants from West Bengal and Tamil Nadu. Bengali and Madrasi lawyers had made monopoly of the legal profession in Odisha. Under the guidance of Mr. P C Chattopadhyay Dad ventured into the legal profession. The relationship between both the mentor and disciple was unique. Mr Chattopadhyay opened the way and revealed the principles, while Dad, as an ardent disciple - meticulously applied, developed and actualized those principles into reality. God's grace, within no time, he was able to surpass his Guru. His mentor was always proud and happy and encouraged him to move on in his chosen profession. As a result of this exquisite bonding and teamwork, the result was achieved. Integrating the teachings in a subtle and profound manner while developing the skills over many years through experience; in course of time Daddy proved his merit and became one of the leading lawyers. Very soon he earned standing in the field of the legal profession for his exceptional intelligence and keen foresightedness.

Normal criminal cases become so fascinating that individuals from different walks of life used to gather in the Court room to hear the proceedings of a case matter. I have heard people say, "while arguing in front of the Judge and opposition party Dad becomes firm, arrogant and fierce to make his point weighty": leading to success.

There are instances when he could solve a petty mystery in his chamber itself. I have heard of the "Drummer", story from my uncle...

One fine morning the native people saw a dead body hanging from the branch of a big Banyan tree just beside the river that flowed in a suburban village close by. This scene caused panic in the area, and the dead body was identified as the famous, "drummer" of that village. When the police reached the place and took care of the body, they detected a gold chain tied to the waist that had a **talisman** attached. Surprisingly, they also spotted a name "Nayana", imprinted on it.

The police immediately identified the drummer who lived in the village. He was very famous in the vicinity. The mystery revolved around the gold chain and who this girl Nayana was that possibly had caused the death of the drummer. Word spread within and around the village to get hold of the girl named, "Nayana". All Nayana-named girls were cross-examined. At last, they found a girl who admitted that the necklace was hers and she had lost it while bathing in the river.

The drummer was a successful professional and had a thriving business; it was clear that on moral grounds he would never steal a gold chain. Again, if he stole the chain why would he commit suicide? Numerous queries remained unsolved. Days passed and the death of the drummer remained a mystery! One fine day, a police van stopped in front of our house. They were serious to solve the drummer's death case. Dad heard each segment of this case. He heaved a sigh of relief and said, "Sympathy in the eyes of a woman, speaks volumes about the epic Ramayana while her desire and will power serves profound enough to create the tides of the Mahabharat." -This could only be a "hearsay", evidence, but it is the absolute truth. He advised the Investigation Agency to bring the girl for further interrogation.

The Police team were not satisfied with this answer of the lawyer. Dad had no time for foul play he immediately ridiculed:

"You, Investigators will keep the key to a locked Almirah in your pocket and will contemplate various ways and means here and there to open the cupboard."

The police squad were convinced; they left for their headquarters.

After a few days, Nayana came to the lawyer's chamber escorted by a team of police men. They were made comfortable, well seated and the grilling began. After a few minutes of silence and provocation Nayana had no other option but to tell the truth.

She admitted a few days ago, she had a rift with her husband and had contemplated to commit suicide. In the middle of the night, she had gone to the bank of the river to give up her life. After a while this drummer had come to the same place completely drunk. Nayana admitted getting scared of the drummer and in panic, told him the reason why she was there at that late hour of the night.

The drummer was drunk and was ready to help her

commit suicide. However, he wanted to take a bribe from Nayana to teach her the skill of hanging from the big banyan tree near the riverside. Highly obliged, fearful, Nayana had offered the drummer her gold necklace. Heavily drunk, the drummer secured the necklace tightly, clinging to his body and with the help of the string of the drum tied himself to the Banyan tree.

---Within minutes the string worked and squeezed the drummer to death. The drunk drummer faced death because of his own folly; Thus, the mystery was resolved! This in fact is only a small episode, revealing my father's detective skills. People marveled and praised his sensible rationale.

He was a man of principles. A true visionary, with deep rooted cultural values besides being a loving father and devoted husband, he fondly cared for his aging father and was an ideal elder brother for his younger siblings. He left no stone unturned to accomplish his duties towards his extended family, neighbors and friends too. Well respected and loved by one and all he stood strong as a "rock".

Blame it on fate!!! He breathed his last in harness. He suffered from a massive heart attack while arguing an important criminal case. In pain he joined his hands and begged for deliverance;" Maa", came to his rescue and he slept in peace. When I look up to Him-he is always there, beside me,,,,,an energetic beam of light and tremendous strength! His smiling face and endearing love for all is etched in my memory forever…so vivid and fresh in my mind's eye.

His untimely death created ripples in the millennium city and adjoining areas. In those days the radio and newspapers were the only means of broadcast. Family and friends were not informed; the news spread like wildfire;

People flocked into our premises to pay their last respect to the noble soul.

A philanthropist by nature, he was a true friend for the poor and needy. Besides being an ardent devotee of Maa Kali, his pragmatic personality with a realistic humble demeanor, he definitely won the hearts of the common people with whom he associated with deep concern and care. For me, my hero! My dear Dad is my biggest role model. I still miss him every day. He imbibed within me so many values and ideals that make me what I am today. To say he was my Superman is an understatement.

-- Proud of my father, his love for his family gave him tremendous courage to achieve the optimum. Highly committed to his profession, he worked tirelessly to pursue his aspirations. A workaholic by nature, unfortunately, he never had the scope to lead an easy-going retired and relaxed life. Knowing his personality for sure, he never aspired to that kind of lifestyle. A pillar of strength for a big joint family, everything seemed to collapse in his absence. The void created remains deep and painful for each one of us.

The experiencing legacy of, "Shri. Bhikari Charan Panda", advocate will continue to inspire and boost our lives endlessly and across generations......

----------- From Thatched Roof to a Beautiful Bungalow was his journey.

Note: *The "Drummer", story is an English translation from an Odiya book, "Bisarna Madhyahna", written by my uncle Mr Gangadhar Tripathy.(Advocate).*

GRANDMA'S GARDEN OF LOVE

Three little flowers blooming bright—
Myra, Diya, and Reya, a joyful sight!
Each one special, unique in their way,
Buzzing around the home in gleeful play.
Lively, naughty, and oh-so-sweet,
They dance to the tunes of their own heartbeat.
Their laughter and cries bring heavenly bliss,
A home filled with love in every kiss.
Myra swears, "Granny is so nice!"
Because she brings me every delight—
Wrapped goodies, crunchy crackers,
And all my favorite sweets in sight!
Diya loves to sit on Grandma's lap,
Eyes wide with wonder, no time for a nap.
She listens to lullabies, odd and loud,
Sung by Granny—off-key but proud!
Reya, the littlest, quiet and calm,
No hidden mischief, only charm.
Her blinking eyes, so soft and bright,
She naps with Granny, holding tight.
Swinging gently, back and forth,
She snuggles close, for all she's worth.
A bear hug warms both heart and soul,

In Grandma's lap, she feels whole.
Grandma's love runs deep and wide,
Etched forever on the heart's inside.
Her love beams up like starlit skies,
Glowing softly where forever lies.
And though I may not be around
To see you grow with feet on ground—
To see you blossom, bold and wise—
Know this truth beneath the skies:
Even if we're far apart,
You'll always live forever, inside my heart.

A NEW LEAF

Arjuna's sorrow in Bhagavad Gita is symbolic of all human suffering. It is out of sorrow and suffering that man becomes interested in philosophical matters and begins his spiritual journey. This may not happen universally, but in most cases it does. Suffering puts ego in its place and forces it to turn to the divine almighty for help, just as Arjuna the great warrior turned to Lord Krishna for divine help and guidance.

Our experiences repeatedly prove that sorrow is the inseparable companion to man, his eye-opener, his true teacher of philosophical truths, without which perhaps he would remain spiritually ignorant.

Kaveri was smart, stubborn and arrogant. She would always describe herself as a winner. She had the ability to pave things in her favor, no matter what the circumstances would be. Today, life has taken a different turn as she stands blank, trying to confront reality.

The wide endless suburban roads of New York seem to have a nostalgic effect on Kaveri. Pleasure trips and work trips along these lanes bring back varied flashbacks from time to time. It is on one of these roads her beloved Avinash had breathed his last, only minutes away from home. Avinash had gone on an errand, and he never returned home. Secured with his seatbelt on, he was found sleeping peacefully, while the car was safely parked in a designated Parking lot. Avinash was no more.

-A saintly person, free from the bondage of worldly entanglements, had closed his eyes forever, flown to His Abode. His cheerful countenance remained a memory, only to be cherished in the minds of many, whose hearts he had touched. As a true partner for Kaveri, he was the balancer making endless compromises in their conjugal life.

-----They were made for each other.

On the same path, months earlier, one day while driving on the road, Kaveri had left him alone to find his way home. It all flickered from a trivial argument that turned into a big brawl inside the car. Ill-tempered, rude selfish and thoughtless as Kaveri was always, she never had second thoughts, The high and mighty had ordered him to step out of her new, "BMW", while she herself had driven back home alone.

Without a word of contempt, Avinash had returned only to forgive his dear wife, ignoring her fault and blaming the devil, for his plight. He calmed himself that his beloved was under the grip of "anger", that shrouds one's thought process, clouding the sense of judgement. Forgive and forget was his attitude in life.

Events like this have occurred many times. Yet, the couple was a perfect match, loved and adored by one and all. The relationship lasted healthily as the following principle was well adhered:

"To keep your marriage brimming,
With love in the loving cup,
Whenever you're wrong admit it:
Whenever you're right shut up"... Ogden Nash

Circumstances have left an indeterminable mark, in the benevolent counsels of time. Today, Kaveri has turned into a new leaf. Now she is willingly available for others, giving a helping hand to neighbors and friends, "Truth", has taught her a lesson that true victory lies in giving, sharing, caring and sacrificing. With a reawakened soul, she strives hard for Self-actualization driven by the strength of past experiences, it's when we put God first in our life that we find the goodness we yearn for.

As per Mahatma Gandhi:

Our peace of mind increases in spite of suffering. We become braver and more enterprising. We understand more clearly the difference between what is everlasting and what is not. We learn to distinguish between what is our duty and what is not. Our pride melts away and we become humble. Our worldly attachments diminish and likewise the evil within us diminishes from day to day.

With a positive frame of mind, kindling the light of Avinash's memory in her heart, she has put God in the center and circumference of all activities. The serene light of goodness envelops her all around. Most of the time, she spends for the benefit of fellow human beings. Time has taught her to serve humanity.

----May the Almighty give her immense strength to overcome her personal loss and share happiness all around.

LOVE

❙❙Love", is that power which sustains life on earth. It can light up a broken heart, it can set ablaze the flame of revenge, it can enlighten young minds as well as proclaim a fiery track for someone who is waiting for a challenge.

The word 'love' comes from the Sanskrit word 'lubhyati', which means 'he desires'. An equivalent of the word and the concept of love appear across all ancient cultures. This profound word is also linked with a hypothetical term "leubh," a root in Proto-Indo-European meaning "care" or "desire". It eventually developed into Latin "libet" and Old English "lufu," both describing deep affection or being very fond of something. The earliest known use of the noun "love" is in the Old English period.

"Love", is an intense feeling. Man, experiences love as his attitude to somebody or something ie. the object of his love. This feeling may differ for different things in the same person. We all feel different about our various love items such as fruit, ice cream, wafers and chips, same as in the case of music and sports, dolls and a pet, spouse and grandparents, child and parents, his home or country. This feeling also differs within each group.

The origin of Love can be traced back to the beginning of creation. The love stories of Laila and Majnu, Romeo and Juliet, of Radha and Krishna are eternal and stand the test of time.

Different schools of thought describe "love" in their own terms:

-Literature: has described love in the form of stories, lyrics and poems that have been encrypted since time immemorial.

-History: is filled with battles of love across regions and territories.

-Mathematics: has helped to add, subtract, and multiply as well as divide love into various styles.

-Geography: has helped bind Love so hard that the world has become a smaller place to live.

-Political Science: true enduring love is built on the edifice of just an agreement that has been laid within the boundaries of constitutional rights.

-Logic: has simply failed to set definitive rules for true love; yet it empowers a person who is engulfed deep within its flames.

-Psychology: the fire of love is crazy; it can make a person go insane….. beyond limits. Strangely, if you are confused about why, you love this person, object or situation; It's Love. For it thrives strongly, in the various states of the mind.

-Sociology: love comprises of basic theories, types, examples and thoughts that form the basis of our socialization process.

-Biology: it drives you mad.

-Statistics: it has infinitive powers.

-Chemistry: fails to analyze it.

-Physics: defines it as a terrific impulse.

-Statistics: reveals; when intensified the power of love rises to the power of infinity.

-Zoology: helps to symbolize love based on its species.

-Economics: true love makes you weak.

-Language: spells the word silently.

-Art: An artist knows how to express it beautifully!

-Computer science: gives one a platform to display love in various ways.

-Artificial intelligence: has taken this strong emotion of love, to a different level altogether. It builds machines that can replicate and replace this intense emotion making human beings redundant.

The common element underlying this love is Man's desire to have the object of his love near him and the fear of losing it. Another common element is the comparableness of the intensity of this feeling with respect to different objects. Everybody usually knows what he loves more and what less, although perhaps not always at once.

All objects of love may be divided into two groups; the "self - love" and the other is "sacrifice". True love is so strong that it forces one to give up and not just to take. This genuine sacrifice somehow reflects on the other person and brings him back to the original force of love.

All the more, true love is born out of self-realization and enlightenment. Here the giver gives without expectation of getting back something in return. Unconditional love begets a lot of joy. Engulfed within the walls of heavenly bliss the person calmly awaits to be rewarded, in unconditional hope!

The basic sense of love is deeply rooted in life on earth. Like the same sense of hunger and thirst this instinct is inherent in both man and animals alike: playing a predominant role in the perpetuation of species.

Strange but true, in addition to the positive feelings romance brings, love also deactivates the neural pathway responsible for negative emotions, such as fear and social judgment. Scientists have proven that both these positive and negative feelings involve two different neurological pathways. When we are engaged in romantic love, the neural machinery responsible for making critical assessments of other people, including assessments of those with whom we are romantically involved, shuts down. "That's the neural basis for the ancient wisdom 'love is blind'," said Schwartz.

Similarly, the love which has developed from long-lasting trust and bonding is more durable than that which arises just from mere attraction. In fact, if the attraction is not reinforced by the strings of friendship it may disappear into thin air like smoke without developing into true "love".

Moreover, proper relations in a family strengthen and consolidate with mutual "love", as the primary force. Precisely this magic wand helps all members work together to strengthen this bond within themselves thereby attaining harmony.

The basic purpose of our life is to surrender to the light of love and receive its warmth deep within our inner soul. The truth lies in the fact that all aspects of human feeling are sweetly combined in profound and intense love, and this is its psychological essence.

......." He Prayuth best who loveth best
All things, both great and small:
For the dear God who loveth us,
He made and loveth all."

- Samuel Taylor Coleridge

REMOTE PAPA- SITTING

// Hello! hi my dear so you are back", I uttered as I eagerly picked up the phone. The voice from the other side had a weary tone. At first, I thought she was just jet-lagged. My dear friend, Rupa, had just returned from India, she had gone to celebrate her Papa's 90th birthday with great enthusiasm and zeal.

"Welcome back home .....I'm sure you had a nice time with Uncle and family in New Delhi. You sound sick, maybe it's just the weather change or sheer tiredness." I expressed my genuine thoughts with concern. Initially, she was hesitant to say anything. After a brief pause, she uttered in a sad tone, "I have to plan and make some arrangement for Dad, the truth lies in the fact that he just can no longer live alone."

"I swear on the Lord, the pictures you shared with me were awesome. Uncle looked mentally emotionally and physically fit. I could foresee no sign of mental or physical ailment in him. I clearly do not understand your concerns." I promptly replied.

Rupa sadly nodded, "the problem lay with the staff. The staff that manages his household is no longer trustworthy. They take him for a ride and do take undue advantage of his genuine goodness. At intermittent intervals they keep demanding a wage hike, unscheduled leaves and on top of it they cheat as and when possible. Those good old days are gone when we used to have trustworthy helpers/care takers."

Living in the US for more than a decade, I always hanker for a helping hand in the house and envy my folks back home who lead a comfy life in India having maids and cooks at their beck and call. Rupa's concern was genuine, and I could relate to her feelings. Getting reliable home help is not an easy task, in the present-day scenario.

I paused, fond memories of Raghukaka/Fakka bhai and Radhikabehen flashed back in memory. These were those family members who helped us in the household. This thought itself brought back nostalgic memories, as they played significant roles in nurturing and caring for us as youngsters. We were attached to them, and they were integral members of our family. Old and frail, Fakka bhai had come in a rickshaw to meet me, when I had visited my hometown after moving to the US- this was our bonding back then.

Rupa's father, at his ripe age, lived alone in their Vasant Vihar bungalow in New Delhi. Rupa, his only child lived in the United States, it was indeed hard for her to look after her father after her mom's untimely death. Dr Narayan was a reputed doctor and had helpers around the house to serve and look after his daily needs.

Rupa had filed for a Green card for her father to stay in the US with her. Unfortunately, her plan did not work out, it was hard for Dr Narayan to adjust to a new life pattern in the US, and he genuinely missed the familiar surroundings back home. He appreciated every little step that Rupa took to take care of him, yet it wasn't practical for him to stay for a long period with Rupa and family. The truth lay in the fact that he had multiple things to take care of back home. Moreover, it wasn't possible to travel consistently every year back and forth, as a result in the process he lost his Green card.

He led a luxurious life in India; he had a cook for giving him fresh homemade meals. A maid to clean the home. A driver, who drove him around in his luxury vehicle. To add to all this, a paid attendant used to come to sleep daily beside him, so that he wasn't left lonely at night. This specially was arranged for him, keeping in view of any emergencies that he might encounter at nighttime.

-Rupa had made all these arrangements meticulously so that every little thing was well taken care of. What else would a dignified man aspire?

Dr Narayan was a benevolent person: kind, generous, and well-meaning. He would often go out of his way to help others and try to do good in the world. Surama, his cook, had looked after him for more than a decade, with a genuine desire to make a positive difference in her life, he had rewarded her with a small LIG flat, close to his bungalow. Very few people with loads of money would hardly take this bold step. This action reveals Dr Narayan's unique personality filled with kindness, gratitude and compassion; he was truly thankful and appreciated her services.

"The solitude of living alone provides an opportunity to know yourself well and become comfortable in your own company," the dignified physician proudly proclaims. Dr Narayan has been living alone for more than 25 years with self-confidence. He sticks to his own routine and enjoys playing bridge with his fellow players. The neighborhood set up is familiar and the people living around give him due respect.

--- Individuals who choose to live alone can experience a greater sense of freedom, control and independence because they can develop an environment and a routine that suits them. It is true: Dr Narayan could manage his household all by himself for so long. However, at this stage of his life, it is naturally becoming tough to micro-manage his household affairs especially with the staff becoming selfish, overconfident and greedy over the years. The truth lies in the fact that the staff had teamed up to cause unnecessary distress and inconvenience for their modest, 'Master'.

Rupa, for the first time during her stay with her father, could sense that things were not working as per the arrangements. Dr Narayan had lost his appetite and was satisfied with simple home-cooked meals. "Surama," the lady who cooked the meals did serve him the required meals in time, but the food was oily and rich. She took special care to train the cook, so that the meals her dad savored were healthy and palatable. Moreover, she discovered the utensils were not in proper shape. It was heart breaking to see the pots and pans covered with a layer of corroded metal linings. This irritated her and she knew that this would adversely affect her father's health. She carefully replaced those utensils with brand new ones of superior quality.

The cleaning lady was smart enough to pick pocket whatever she could and take them home at the slightest opportunity. Be it a small steel bowl, a set of unused cutleries or some leftover coins or currency. Things were constantly missing from home. Keeping every small item under lock and key was not a suitable option. Problems like this were not only irritating, but it was also not easy for Dr Narayan to deal with such nuisances from time to time.

The driver, who was supposed to drive him around would constantly overcharge him on bills for minor car repair episodes. It is a shame to relate that he had the audacity to use Dr Narayan's car to teach driving lessons to enthusiastic youngsters who would pay him for that, this was done cleverly without the knowledge of the rightful owner. Despite being an educated family man with proper means, he took advantage of Dr Narayan at the slightest opportunity. Hitches like this were a constant worry for Dr Narayan.

Such incidents were still tolerable. The climax was reached when things turned from bad to worse. It was hard for me to digest when I heard the sickening story that occurred at home, in the absence of the Master.

It so happened; Dr Narayan had left his home and had gone to spend a week with a friend who lived in Shimla. Assuming the staff would look after his home in his absence, he had just locked his bedroom and left. He in fact had made sure that his staff would not face any inconvenience while he was away.

This opportunity gave the night watchman along with the driver to have a gala time at home in the absence of the Master. They brought in bottles of alcohol and had real fun time with the two ladies. Surprisingly, the staff had the cheek to indulge in unsociable behavior while on duty!

On his return, Dr Narayan could sense that Surama the cook was still in a delirious state and could barely stand upright. He immediately made all arrangements and sent her to the Primary Local Health Care Centre for proper treatment.

This was the ultimatum, Rupa also did her own investigation; everything was apparent after she unwind the camera from her Atlanta residence and could herself better gauge the gravity of the situation. She realized that the present planning for her father was no longer suitable, and other options should be considered as an alternative.

As an outsider, it was very much obvious that it was none of my business to poke into Rupa's personal matters. As a good friend, I just could not stay quiet. The next day, when I spoke to her very politely, I queried, "Rupa, u have a lot of extended family in New Delhi, why can't you ask them for help. I am sure someone could help in a positive way."

Sadly, Rupa replied, "I have tried that path too, these days everyone is burdened with their own troubles, no one has the time and energy for others; be it relatives or friends. This is what it is, and I must tackle this situation myself."

Her words left an impending mark on my mind, I felt sad and disturbed; in no way could I help alleviate Rupa's burden! Thoughts kept pondering yet the solution was nowhere to be found. I folded my hands and thanked God for giving me kind and responsible siblings to care for my parents back in India while I lived a carefree life in the United States of America.

After a few days I met Rupa in the club house, she just wasn't her normal self. I could sense an apprehensive look on Rupa's face. Trying to be caring and helpful, in a positive way, I suggested that she should look up assisted living facilities for Uncle in India. Rupa did agree that she had already done enough research: looking for a luxury retirement home with state-of-the-art facilities for her father. But, with a pause, she said:" the time for that arrangement is still far away. Right now, I desperately want to honor my Dad's wish to live independently in his own home as long as he can. He really does not want to leave his home. All his memories are deeply etched within the four walls of that house, and he sincerely cherishes the settings", Rupa explained.

The best alternative for her was to become the online

caretaker of her father, supervising each minute detail of activities from afar. Of course, that was possible with proper coordination. With access to modern day online facilities, every day she started taking special pains to monitor the activities of the staff. It was not an easy task, yet it was doable.

----Where there's a will, there's a way! The Lord helped Rupa in caring for her dear Dad, as best as she could. Differences in time did pose as a stumbling block, however this arrangement worked like magic, The strings were in Rupa's hands. The staff was more co-operative and organized.

At each and every opportunity - in frequent intervals she would fly all the way to be physically present with her beloved "Papa". Today, technology is Power: our ultimate savior.

-"A father's tears and fears are unseen, his love is unexpressed, but his care and protection remain as a pillar of strength. My father didn't tell me how to live. He lived and let me watch him do it."

-Anonymous-

SELF ENLIGHTENED

It was a beautiful bright Sunday when this happened, on that fateful morning   of March 2nd 2022. Nothing was new, Kirti had just finished sipping her morning cup of coffee; she could hear Rajiv's heavy footsteps proceeding towards her. She was very familiar with her hubby's delirious actions. It was normal, and she was pretty used to the drama.

Rajiv walked towards the Bar; he grabbed the vodka bottle from the shelf and poured himself a glass. Kirti could hear him gulping the aerated drink in a jiffy. Her dear husband looked fierce. With an uncontrollable swing of his fist, he spit out angrily: "in this home either I stay or you, time to decide. Seriously, I want a divorce. Today, I am leaving you forever," he frowned.

It wasn't easy to digest such nasty words. Kirti, however, had learned to stay cool. She had understood the hard way to accept her circumstances and quietly made a conscious commitment and decision to let things go.

Kirti had met him on the school campus. He was a year senior, tall, handsome with a smart appearance....... a perfect fiancé. Friends envied the cute pair. He was a US citizen and Kirti was a F1 visa student from the capital city of India.

The courtship period was a dream come true for Kirti. Going out together and enjoying the beauty of Mega

Manhattan city was just part of the fairytale. Rajiv had the means to squander money for every little thing that Kirti appreciated. His benevolent actions were noteworthy. She soon became more and more comfortable; they started taking short pleasure trips. The trip to Niagara Falls was captivating, the scenic atmosphere was a perfect backdrop; Rajiv proposed, and she lovingly accepted the alliance. In fact, Kirti was emotionally swept away from her feet. Amidst the trance that she was engulfed within, she shyly succumbed to the connection.

Kirti was wary and scared when it was time to tell her parents about all the exciting developments that had taken place in her life. Her parents were happy with the proposal and had an instant liking for their would-be son -in -law. One thing that bothered them was that they never had wanted their only daughter to settle down in such a far-off land away from home. Studying and getting a US degree was their primary goal and nothing beyond that. Marching out into the world with a Cornell degree was an asset, it would not only serve as a steppingstone to getting a better job in her field but also broaden her outlook in dealing with life's unpredictable twists and turns.

Kirti started to dream about settling in the US and having a perfect family. Rajiv had introduced Kirti to his parents and they had accepted her wholeheartedly. Happy days rolled on for both and soon Rajiv graduated from college. He started working with his father in the family enterprise. In the meantime, Kirti also finished her degree course and started looking for a job in her domain of study. Getting a perfect job with her current visa status was not easy. Both decided that it was time to settle down. Rajiv was an American citizen, consequent upon their marriage Kirti would be eligible for a Green Card. Armored with a valid work permit things would work better for Kirti, thus steering her career path.

A grand wedding was planned in a resort for the loving couple in Agra. The focus was to give Rajiv's family and friends the perfect opportunity to savor the beauty of Taj Mahal in Agra while participating in the core wedding ceremony. Each event was well planned and tailor made with care and precision. The wedding bells rang in fervor and pronounced them as a perfect couple.

Visa issues posed as a stumbling block, Kirti had to stay back with her parents, while Rajiv came back to join his work. The long-distance relationship was painful and lasted for three long years. During those years of exile, they would make sure to meet up either in India or in Canada. Getting into the US was difficult for Kirti.

In course of time, Kirti became a legitimate green card holder and her entry to the US was facilitated. Both the partners were excited, and they dreamt of starting their life together. Rajiv flew to New Delhi to bring Kirti home.

It was the saddest goodbye at the airport as Kirti hugged her parents. Her parents also stood unhappy, feeling the weary weight of solitude, watching their child leave, their hearts heavy with love and hope.

Kirti was given a warm welcome in the Kejriwal residence, very much in the traditional Indian way. The home atmosphere was cozy, and everything worked in their favor. Her father-in-law's welcome note kept ringing in Kirti's ears:

"It's great to have you with us! We're excited for the journey together as we march ahead and all the blessings that are to come." – A. P. Kejriwal

At first, everything felt like a dream---

Kirti admitted the feeling was heavenly! "Novelty,

all around me, I hoped against hopes for a new beginning loaded with love and acceptance." After a deep pause, writhing with a deep sigh of sadness she moaned, "unfortunately...... my dream started to crack ".

In the course of time, expectations arose, and Kirti had no answer to the queries that kept bombarding her from time to time. At times it would get into her nerves, and she would get irritated. Sadly, the elderly parents were very much outdated in their beliefs and thought patterns and had the same mindset that Indian society had almost forty years back when they had left India. Modern India for sure has a new facelift. Thoughts, feelings and the general outlook have changed for the better suiting to the tunes of tech savvy progressive youngsters.

Every fortnight at Intervals Rajiv used to go out on a business trip and would come back home after a gap of five days. At first it was hard for Kirti to figure it out, his behavior at home was different. This happened mostly after his return from the trip. She sensed something unusual and fishy.

Six years had passed, and the young couple were still childless, everyone was worried and of course the blame was on Kirti. Bhavna, her sister-in -law had two beautiful kids; they would come home at frequent intervals. The kids were adorable; the elders doted on them. Poor Kirti was taunted for being childless; the blame was always on the daughter-in-law, adding fuel to the fire. Even Bhavna did not hesitate to mock and torment Kirti, because of her inability to have a child. Gradually, Kirti became sadder and more depressed. At times, she would repent leaving her loving family in India and coming all the way to settle down in the US.

Rajiv unfortunately, had no voice in family matters

and hardly showed any support to his distressed wife. Frequent trips to the doctor's office proved to be futile. Kirti chose to focus herself on her job and career rather than being involved in foolish family gimmicks.

She missed the warmth of her native country and longed for the love of her parents. The pain of staying far from near and dear ones affected her dreams of the charm of living a happy life in the US, she felt as if she was chained to a ship lacking a safe harbor.

For sure, she knew Rajiv, and it was her conscious decision to become his life partner. She realized that everything looked rosy in the dating era. Later, it was apparent that Rajiv was not only a Mama's boy, with certain narcissistic traits but a victim of drugs.

Kirti, felt helpless; "The man I trusted- my husband, my shield….. chose to be silent. I missed the MAN, I loved. "At times she felt like eloping from the scene and take refuge within the haven of her Parents' home.

"Oh no! "She exclaimed. Kirti, often spoke to herself and her inner voice served as a guide for future actions. Upsetting the present set up was not the solution, her will power made her stronger to tackle the scenario with dignity. ---She was a cultured and determined lady, she very well knew that sharing her sorrow with her parents would take her nowhere. This was her house; wherein she would strive to grasp her foothold. She remained calm and composed; despite being fully aware that she was treading on thin ice. She decided to deal with her husband with the utmost empathy and set perfect boundaries as per the situation.

Her conversations with her parents were normal, Kirti made sure never to share her worries with them. Silently she prayed to Maa Durga for her divine blessings! Auto suggestion and self-therapy made her stronger day by day. She understood, this was her home, and she had to learn to live with dignity despite the odds. Instead of whining and moaning about the circumstances, she learned to direct her own energy deep within .....thus diverting the attained energy into her own light.

Kirti's first step was focused on the art of self-love. This helped her to maintain kindness in her relationship with the family. Tactfully and slowly with sweet words, actions of love and compassion, she practiced the art of mindful communication with all the members that lived with her in that home. Her commitment to improving a healthy and lasting relationship grew stronger day by day. Slowly she could perceive the change, an invisible warmth of peace, which served as bonding; soon engulfed the four walls of the Kejriwal residence. This commitment involved being proactive in addressing issues, seeking new ways to connect, and continuously striving to be kind and understanding with each other.

Kirti was a blessing for their home. Her loyalty to continuous improvement served as an essential aspect of a healthy and lasting relationship. Utilizing strong proactive thoughts Kirti would regularly assess and work on the relationship ties, thus ensuring that it remained strong and resilient.

Kirti cultivated mindfulness, she started nurturing connections with others that brought joy and fulfillment in her life. She prioritized self-care, understanding to take care of herself both physically and mentally. She made time for activities that recharged and rejuvenated her body and mind such as gardening and enjoying long walks along scenic surroundings. Soon she was able to radiate happiness, wherever she went. Last but not the least she never forgot to make gratitude a daily practice. She took time each day to reflect on the little joys she was thankful for, whether it was appreciating the flowers blooming in the garden, bird watching or just playing with the maid's kid. Soon, by consciously focusing on the positive aspects of life, she was able to cultivate a mindset of abundance and appreciation that fueled her happiness. Nurturing connections with family was the key! The laughter of loved ones or the simple pleasures of life literally transformed the social set up.

-God bless Kirti with a happy family life!

---"Maintaining kindness in a relationship, especially during conflicts, is crucial for its long-term success."

-*Anonymous*-

LEARNING-LIFE LESSONS

Living in a quiet town, in the suburbs of New York many times I miss the hustle bustle and the crowd of Cuttack, the ancient city in which I grew up. Here in winters, everyone is packed inside their cozy homes, so it is all the drearier and bleaker. ......Winter blues!

Last night I had gone to pick up my husband from the train station (Ossining) at 7:30pm. As soon as I parked my car at the boarding point, a hefty well-dressed guy came close to the car, before I could realize what was happening, he opened the back door and was comfortably seated at the rear seat.

My first instinct; I grabbed my purse and ran out of the car. Obviously, it was pitch dark and the station was deserted. Fortunately, I could see a lady at the end of the downhill road. I ran as fast as my stout legs could carry me, screaming for HELP! She heard me and came rushing to me, I gained confidence with her presence. My phone was in my hand; with trembling fingers I could not dial 911. My angel did it, (the lady) lo! within half a minute the cops came. Hats off to the timely service of the POLICE DEPARTMENT.

The intruder was still seated inside the car; after seeing the police he opened the door and came out with a confused look on his face. Poor guy, he was intoxicated and can u guess what he thought?

For him I was the UBER guy for whom he had been waiting for a while.

A lesson learnt:

Always be aware of your surroundings. Twenty years I have lived in this town and have picked up family members at odd hrs. of the night. An unforgettable experience. God sent an angel for me right in time of need, His blessings…... all well that ends well. HE is our, "savior".

BLESSINGS!

Happy birthday my dear Son,

- Time has indeed flown by so fast. You are still my little one my dear! So happy, you have reached a milestone, "Forty"!

Suprav, our little Ganesha has grown up to be a responsible adult. Our dreams have come true! Nikki, our daughter-in- law, is a perfect life partner for him. She is loving, sweet and a multitasking queen who has planned this celebration with ease. Myra and Reya are precious cute girls gifted to us from heaven. Take care of each other and move on ....keep working hard to build a brighter future for the little ones.

As you celebrate this important day of your life, we proudly claim our dear little babe has grown into an amazing Man of "essence". Your journey inspires us, and we are grateful for the varied experiences that have shaped you.

Life truly begins here as you blossom into your "Forties". It's time to look back and reflect on all your achievements so far. Precious are the kids who have made your life more meaningful, thank God for the togetherness and love for each other. Grateful; for all things big and small that u have achieved so far.

----Dream big and deep, as your understanding of yourself and the relationships around is more mature. Now you are free to make new choices to become someone who works better for yourself in this world.

Praying for your well-being as life unfolds, our Blessings are always with you.....strong enough to guide you and make all your visions true. You have filled our lives with meaning and that love for you just grows deeper and stronger with time.

_____Love you …. "Beta"!

Blessings and love,

"MAA"

Black Eagle Books

www.blackeaglebooks.org
info@blackeaglebooks.org

Black Eagle Books, an independent publisher, was founded
as a nonprofit organization in April, 2019. It is our mission
to connect and engage the Indian diaspora and the world at
large with the best of works of world literature published
on a collaborative platform, with special emphasis on
foregrounding Contemporary Classics and New Writing.